THE KILL TOUCH

HAVILAH G

THE WHUMPY PRINTING PRESS

Cover Illustration by Hen Towers

Cover Design by Nicole Alessi

ALSO BY HAVILAH G

The Ghost of Seattle

Dance of Death

Miasma

Mighty

Back to the Dregs

CONTENTS

—·—

CONTENT WARNINGS

This story contains the following content:
- Teenage protagonist

- Death of parents

- Blood, violence, torture

- Captivity

- Restraints

If this book isn't for you, no worries! But if it is, we hope you enjoy this story about a sarcastic, electrokinetic girl...

THE KILL TOUCH

Y'Starren's family trudged down the walking path to Wenterglen, where Strangers' College nestled; a beacon of hope. They had been wanderers for most of her life, and when they weren't actively running from police, they were pretty happy. But Strangers' College was supposed to be a safe haven for people like them.

Everyone in her family had the gift of electrokinesis – what most people called "the Kill Touch." If only they'd been born with something stupid like clairvoyance or illusions, they could've lived in peace. But instead, her family had the unique ability to cause extreme pain, or even kill, using electrokinesis. Every time someone found out about them, they had to move on from that town. No one was comfortable with someone that could kill just by touching them, and her parents had had to fend off several pitchfork-wielding mobs and even a few assassins already.

Still, when they were together and felt safe-ish, like right now, life was great.

"I'm so hungry," Wackee complained, doing a little dance of hunger as he rubbed his stomach.

"Like that's going to help." Mother ruffled his hair good-naturedly. "Put some pressure on your stomach."

Wackee groaned.

"It hurts, Mother, that's just going to make it worse."

Y'Starren focused away from her own knotted-up stomach, listening to the birds around them, watching for wildlife, admiring the golden morning sunlight shining through the leaves. It made a spotted, twinkling pattern on the forest path that their bare feet tramped over.

"Just keep an eye out," her father said, walking at the front with his anxious eyes shifting through the foliage for predators, assassins, Ghost Men, or whatever else he was worried about at the moment.

Suddenly Wackee let out a squeal and dashed forward and to the side of the path, crashing into the underbrush with a roar of excitement.

"What's wrong?" Father shouted.

Y'Starren jogged forward hopefully.

"Apples! Apples!" Wackee screamed back at them.

Y'Starren broke into a run after him, following him down a tiny little rabbit trail into a meadow. How he'd seen it from the main trail was a mystery to her.

He was already rooting around among the apples on the ground like a wild animal, throwing them behind himself, crawling forward.

"That one's rotten. That one's wormy. That one's rotten and wormy ... "

"So pick from the tree." Y'Starren rolled her eyes, picking one from the sagging branch nearby and tossing it in front of Wackee.

He pounced on it with his whole body, and she heard a crack as he bit into it recklessly.

"Horizons," he cursed through his bites. "It's delicious."

There were so many apples. Y'Starren was going to dream of apples that night, she just knew it. Heavy clusters of palm-sized red and green apples weighed down the thick branches, making them droop low enough into the meadow for her family to grab to fill their packs.

"We could make apple pie," Mother commented as she gathered them into her basket.

"Oh, fuck yes!" Wackee roared from inside the tree, mouth still very full.

"It's bad luck to strip the tree," Father called from where he sat in the branches, trying to boost her little brother up to grab the higher apples. "Make sure you leave some for the next travelers."

"Tell that to Wackee," Y'Starren said, picking a final apple to eat as she lay back on the grass. It's always better to eat while you're watching the clouds.

"Now all we have to do is find somewhere safe to camp tonight," Father said.

***

Something told Y'Starren that she was alone.

Her eyes flashed open and she rolled out of the bundle of blankets she'd shared with her little brother last night. She looked around in the shack they'd used to camp in the last leg of their journey to Strangers' College, training her ears to the outside.

Besides the birds and breeze through the underbrush, there was nothing.

The orange-haired girl jumped up, grabbing a cloak and fastening the buttons as she thought.

Had they decided to go ahead to the college without her?

"Like Wackee's the only one going ... " she grumbled. "And he forgot his papers. Again."

She grabbed them and stuffed them into her tunic as she dashed out the front of the shack.

"Guys?" she called. "Wackee?" she called for her crazy twelve-year-old little brother.

5

Nothing.

She pulled her hood over the dread-like braids she'd left in her hair overnight; it was cold on the trail as she hurried up the mountainside.

For the first time in her family's history, they'd had a hope of living somewhere that their gifts would be considered normal.

"If they've ruined my introduction to Strangers' College, I'm going to be mad," Y'Starren muttered, hurrying down the path. Maybe they were just exploring. Without her.

The forest near Wenterglen turned out to be pretty damp in the springtime. Y'Starren buttoned her cloak further down over her arms, huddling deep under the hood for warmth.

Y'Starren followed the tiny trail to a meadow, where it disappeared among the grass and stumps of trees.

"Wackee?" Y'Starren shouted. "Guys? This better just be an unusually bad case of diarrhea. There's no other reason to go this far without telling me where you went!"

She heard no response, and was about to turn back when she saw a dark shape at the opposite end of the meadow.

Clutching her cloak around her with a frown, she moved toward the creature. Suddenly it broke from the forest and darted in her direction. It was a man in black and white, and he was holding a sword. She started back, but then she raised both hands, snapping her fingers. Magic cracked in the air between her fingers as she glared into the man's eyes – it was a warning.

The moment the man saw that, he veered away from her with a frightened look in his eyes.

She knew that look, and laughed a little.

That was the look of a Clairvoyant who had met with an unforeseen circumstance.

She heard him slow down in the bushes just past the clearing, panting and moving around, probably adjusting his position to prepare for a better offense.

"Hey, mister," she called. "You alone?"

He didn't answer.

"If you're alone, think again," she said. "And put that sword back in your pants."

She heard him stand up and the sound of a sword going back into a wooden scabbard. Then she heard him sigh and mutter, and then tramp away through the woods.

This close to barbarian land, it was pretty normal for people to go around with weapons, but Y'Starren didn't like it.

She tucked her cold hands back under her warm cloak and kept walking toward a larger hill. Wackee had begged to go there on a picnic today, and Y'Starren wondered if that was where he was.

As she reached the foot and climbed out of the brush onto another trail, she saw him.

He was standing there, without a cloak, without even a pouch, as if he'd just climbed out of bed and run into the woods.

And he was standing in front of their mother on the ground, eyes fixed on her, blood all over his hands.

"Wackee?" she said. "What happened?"

He stared at their mother as if he didn't see or hear Y'Starren.

Y'Starren knew what she'd see if she looked down, somehow.

Her mother's wide eyes were staring into the treetops, unseeing, yet somehow shocked.

"Where's Dad?" Y'Starren said, finding herself going numb in the face with a sense of shock.

As she pulled stray hair from her face, her hood fell back, allowing the bracing mountain air to whip around her cheeks. They stung. She was crying. "Where's Dad?" she repeated. "Wackee, what did you do?"

Finally, Wackee's arm moved; he pointed to the left.

Their father was face-down in the bushes a bit further off. Y'Starren softly stepped over to him, knelt and touched his bare shoulder, then flinched back. It was like cold, hard clay.

"Are they gonna be alright?" Wackee said, and his voice was husky like he'd already screamed several times. Y'Starren felt horrible for not having heard it.

"How would they be alright?" she said. "They're dead."

That was when Wackee broke into a horrified groan, and Y'Starren pulled him away from their parents, wrapping her cloak around him, trapping him in a hug.

"It'll be okay, it'll be okay," she comforted him. She didn't know why she was saying it, but it was all she could think of to say. "We'll be okay."

At that, he cried even louder.

"Wackee, stop it. Stop it," she said. "I saw a guy coming my way with a sword. Did you see what happened?"

As he continued to cry and not answer, she glanced over her little brother's shoulders and looked at the wounds on her mother's neck again.

A sword could easily do that, she thought. But then, so could any sharp object, probably. She wasn't sure. "Wackee, a guy with mud-color hair. Angry eyes. Did you see him?"

Wackee kept crying.

"Were you here when they ... When did you get here?"

Wackee shook his head.

"I didn't," he cried. "I was too late."

Y'Starren let out a small breath of relief.

It didn't feel exactly real that they could be gone. She felt like she could just take him back to their old town and they'd find their parents waiting at home for them, like they always used to.

At the same time, the present reality did make sense. Rather than seek to imprison such dangerous, gifted citizens, the government would probably prefer to simply assassinate them. Which meant that if that man Y'Starren had seen was the assassin, she was next. He couldn't possibly know about Wackee, or he would've killed him when he got to their parents. Better keep Wackee a secret, then.

"Wackee, I need you to do something for me," she said, releasing her brother.

He looked over his shoulder at his parents on the ground.

"No, Wackee – " She pushed his shoulder and dragged him away from the spot. "Come on. Let's pretend."

"I'm not in the mood!" he said.

"Wackee," she said, pulling him along. "Let's say that they're back in Seechatee. Okay? They sent us – they sent you to the college. They already paid for your first three months."

"I don't understand ... " He sniffled, wiping his nose on his hand, then wiping his hand all over his shirt.

It was true that they'd already paid the first three months at Strangers' College in advance for both kids. But if Y'Starren went there with him, she'd only draw assassins after both of them. Besides, they'd have nothing to do after three months.

"I'm going to get a job in Wenterglen," she said. "You're going to Strangers' College."

"You're gonna leave me?" He covered his mouth to keep from crying anymore. "How could you – don't leave me!"

She stopped and wrapped him in a hug again.

"I'll visit you," she said. "But if I come, then ... " She didn't want to scare him.

"Then what?"

"Look, I'll explain later," she said. "Now you better trust me. You go to the college and show them your papers."

"Will you come with me?"

"I can't."

He looked at her with his big eyes, legs trembling like he might just collapse.

"You can take care of yourself," she said. "I know you can. I have to go report the murder to the Investigator's Guild. Okay?"

She hoped he'd take the bait and stay in safety while she figured out who the killer was. It had to be someone in the guild, if they were local.

"I'll just wait for you," he said, turning toward the shack, which was now in sight.

"Not that way," she said. "Here." She pressed his papers into his hand, which she'd grabbed for him on the way, just in case they'd already gone straight for the college and forgotten them.

"Go straight to the college. I'll see you there tonight."

Finally, he listened to her and tromped off toward the college.

Y'Starren sighed as she watched him go, then suddenly her knees gave out and she sank back against a large clattery bush, which crackled under her as she leaned back.

"Oh, fuck," she whispered as the realization of what she'd seen began to sink in. She was going to cry for real; she could feel it gathering with the heat in her face. "Fuck."

***

Y'Starren arrived at the Investigator's Guild hot and tired, cloak pulled back over her shoulders with her orange hair even more windblown than before. She hadn't had the energy to re-braid her hair on the way, as she normally would have.

Her face ached from the set expression that wouldn't change since the moment she'd separated from Wackee.

The Investigator's Guild had a front lobby that felt like it was outside; light shafted down through the huge openings under upper arches made of weathered wood, and the roof had a hole right in the middle. A large stage for a bard rose up all bare and lonely in the middle of the day, and only a few investigators were even there.

As she paused, wondering who to speak to, several of them got up from nearby tables. One of them, a man with a barbarically brown tint to his orange hair, got up with a generous smile and sauntered over to her, followed by two others from the same table.

They wore black coats and white waistcoats, which had completely gone out of fashion for everyone except for people in the government.

Suddenly she stiffened and stared at the man with the brownish hair. He was the guy she'd brushed by in the forest earlier today.

She tilted her head.

He tilted his head in the opposite direction.

"Do I recognize you?" he said, squinting. "Are you the one that snapped your fingers at me this morning in the woods?"

"You ... " She hesitated, realizing that if he was, she was in danger. Someone who killed her parents for their gift would absolutely be coming for her next.

"Who's in charge here?" she said instead of finishing her accusation.

"I am." The dangerous man folded his arms.

"The half-barbarian is in charge," she said, not smiling. "Yeah, right. I'm surprised they haven't deported you yet."

As she said that, a dark scowl overtook his face and he stepped toward her, hand on the hilt of his sword.

But a man behind him with white hair and a young face put his hand on the half-barbarian's shoulder, stepping out in front of him and extending his other hand to Y'Starren.

"Merreth, she asked who's in charge," he said as she shook it. "I'm Relleck. Constant. You?"

A Constant's gift was to live longer and heal more quickly. They developed white hair and kept their youthful-looking faces for most of their lives.

"Y'Starren," she said, finding herself unable to smile. "So, I came here to ask you to investigate a murder, but ... "

Her stern orange eyes rested on Merreth as a bitter grimace came over her face.

Merreth scowled deeper at her and he laid his hand on his sword. Y'Starren lifted her hand, magic running between her fingers, but then Relleck thrust his hand behind himself and pushed the sword back into the scabbard.

"Relleck. She's the other target," Merreth said.

At that, heads perked up around the room. Y'Starren heard people outside moving closer, blocking the entryway. But her head was beginning to buzz with magic and adrenaline. Nothing mattered except this man standing before her – the man who had killed her parents.

"The fuck did you just say?" she said, stepping toward him.

He stepped backward, drawing his sword.

"Don't make yourself a murderer, girl," Relleck said from behind her.

Y'Starren wasn't even listening. She stared down her parents' killer, eyes wide.

"Come on, girl, snap your fingers for me," Merreth said.

"Oh, trust me, you don't want me to do that," she said, appraising the investigators outside, blocking her exit. They weren't even scared.

"I dare you," he said, advancing on her with his sword.

She cursed and stopped as she reached the door. She'd never had to hurt anyone before. She wasn't sure she could. She glared.

Then she raised her hand and snapped her fingers.

Magic arced out from her fingertips, down Merreth's sword, and arced over the leather-wrapped hilt to his hand. The sword clattered to the ground.

"Ah! Fuck!" He shook and wrung his hand.

At that moment, she felt a yank on one of her braids. She spun around, igniting with anger, and clamped a hand over her attacker's, sending magic into them.

She felt it climb up their arm and hit them in the chest, knocking them backward several steps, and they fell to the ground.

"Do not," she shouted, "*touch* the hair!"

The others began to surround her more warily now, gripping their weapons tightly.

She cursed and backed against the wall as the other investigators from outside the front of the guild came inside, holding crossbows. As they got closer, she lowered her hands and stood up straight, as straight as she could, looking around with a hard expression.

A woman behind Y'Starren laid a hand on her shoulder. Y'Starren spun around and pointed two fingers at the woman's forehead. She pulled her in front of her chest quickly, a shield for the crossbow bolts, she hoped. She had seen one up to the feathers in a deer's chest before, so she wasn't sure it would work, but maybe they'd think twice about killing another investigator.

The other investigators got closer and closer, jumping in, but then jumping back just before she touched them.

Snap-snap-snap.

Each snap arced out a few inches into a reaching hand, a sword, a dagger, and jumped into their bodies.

They screamed, and some of them fell suddenly or dropped their weapons. Most of what Y'Starren could do was to inflict pain, and she hated it.

"I told you, you don't want me to." She panted, holding up her left hand threateningly over her lowered head, fingers still pointed at the woman's temple. She could feel her magic skittering between her fingertips, hotter than the blood rushing through her head.

"Go ahead and shoot!" Merreth shouted, slashing down toward her with his sword.

"Don't you dare!" Y'Starren shouted. "I will kill this woman."

"Don't … " the woman whimpered. "I'm sorry. I didn't mean to offend you, I was just trying to do my job. Please, please don't hurt me."

"Shut up or I will," Y'Starren lied through her teeth. The woman's pleading was wrenching her heart, and she couldn't afford to look indecisive right now.

The others around her had paused when Y'Starren made her threats. She could hear the crossbowmen above her whispering to each other –

"Do we … Do we do it?"

She glanced up to see one of them vigorously shaking his head.

Y'Starren put her hand back down on the hostage's shoulder.

"Please ... " the woman whispered, shaking in fear.

"Shh," Y'Starren said under her breath into the woman's ear. "Calm down."

The woman was about the same age as Y'Starren's mother had been. Y'Starren bit her cheek, keeping her face stuck in that resolute expression that had been frozen on her.

"I will do it – I will kill her," Y'Starren said, more loudly. "So nobody shoot me if you want this woman to live."

There was a silence and Y'Starren heard people moving behind her, around the corner where she couldn't see.

"Don't hurt her, please," Relleck said, hands out pacifyingly. "Please. Don't make yourself a murderer."

Y'Starren looked over to the surrounding guild members. They were dangerous – these were the highest-trained police in the entire country of Baneon. Even the woman she had her fingers pointed at was glaring at her as if she'd already accepted that this job was going to get her killed.

At this point, she wasn't going to convince them that she wasn't dangerous, which meant that as soon as she was subdued, they'd certainly execute her. Baneon had no prison system – it was basically liberation, deportation, or death.

But she also knew that one of the most popular things to do with criminals was to work out a deal with them to benefit society in some way, which meant they might be interested in an agreement of some kind ...

"Hey." Y'Starren licked her lips. "So, yeah, you think I'm a danger." She looked around. Now that she had gathered her wits a bit, she could see the terror more plainly on their faces. Like everyone else who had ever heard about what her family could do, they were scared.

"So, this is me when I'm trying not to hurt anyone," she said. "But we don't have to be enemies ... How about this: give me a job here."

She'd been looking for a job in the city anyway, to pay for Wackee's protection at the college. Not this job, but ...

"I'm tough, and I've got the most powerful gift in the world," she said. "Sure you don't want to use that? You hire me, you ... " She hesitated, realizing they had relaxed a bit and were looking at each other with more interest in their eyes. "You hire me, you get to see what I can do for you when I'm serious."

"You have a job." Relleck was the first to step forward and extend his hand.

Y'Starren released the woman with a muttered apology and a pat on the shoulder, which made her flinch.

She stepped forward and shook Relleck's hand.

"Thanks," she said gravely. "Honestly, I have nowhere else to go. Now that my parents are dead."

She turned her icy gaze on Merreth. He raised his hands in an exaggerated shrug.

"I didn't do it," he said.

"Didn't do it, bullshit!" Y'Starren spat. "I – I saw you!"

"I just happened to be there, traveling through the area," he said, then rubbed his jaw thoughtfully. Maybe he was coming up with some more bullshit. "I was looking for your family, but not to kill you. I'm so sorry for your loss."

Y'Starren glared at him, wracking her brains. Should she believe him? How could she know for sure?

"If you're going to be working with Merreth, you need to make peace with him," Relleck said, folding his arms.

Not completely convinced, Y'Starren frowned at the floor. Her chest started to heave as she thought about her parents, and she blinked back the tears and looked up at the bit of sky visible through the small vents at the top of the arched ceiling, trying to keep from crying.

"Right," she sniffed, and nodded after a moment. "Of course I am."

***

Two days later, Y'Starren was alone, swinging a sword at a practice dummy but too afraid to actually hit it, because it looked kind of like a person. A person that hadn't ever done her any harm; an innocent bystander.

She paused, lowering her sword at the dummy and walking up to it.

"You know, you look a little beat up," she said to it. "If I had my way, I'd sit you down and get you a nice flask of tea. We'd go over there up the hill, sit down on that bench, and watch the sunset. You could show me your scars. I'd tell you about my little – "

She was interrupted by a quick *woosh* that ended in a blow to her shoulder. She clutched her shoulder and spun around, sputtering curses.

It was Merreth, and he was swinging the stick again in the direction of her head. She blocked and took the blow on her forearm.

"Motherfucker!" she shouted.

"Pick up your sword," he said, pointing the stick at her. "Let's see how well you fight."

"It's been two days, asshole," Y'Starren growled, arm throbbing now. "Horizons, do you even know how to be nice?"

"It seems you've got enough niceness for both of us," he said, glancing at the dummy behind her. "Looks like you're making friends already."

"I take what I can get." She shrugged, picking up her sword. "Now leave me alone."

"Make me."

***

Y'Starren yanked the visitor's chair away from Relleck's desk by the arm and sat down hard with a huff, glaring at Relleck.

"I'd ask you not to act like you were raised in a barn, but – "

"But I was." Y'Starren rolled her eyes. "Look." She pointed at the fresh bruise on her arm. "He hurt me. Again."

Y'Starren hadn't had a moment to rest since starting her job. She'd been too worried about being followed to try to visit Wackee – she couldn't have Merreth finding out about her little brother, just in case he really was the assassin.

And she'd been being pushed to learn how to fight by the guild trainer, and fitted for some investigator clothing, and introduced to some serious rivalry in the guild. Apparently no one under twenty-three had ever joined the guild before, and almost everyone here had about ten years of experience refining their gifts, going through training academies, often with a background in police work. The investigators were the best of the best, often hand-picked by a king to join the guild.

Apparently they saw Y'Starren as someone who had been dealt a good hand that she totally didn't deserve. It pissed her off. But at least she didn't have time to think about her troubles, with all the stress of her new position.

"I don't care about your little bruise." Relleck sighed. "You're supposed to be practicing fighting. And I'm very blazing busy, so please get out of my – "

"In what world is a two-hundred-pound man beating up a teenager acceptable?"

"So just--zap him a little."

" ... I can't." Y'Starren sighed uncomfortably and looked out Relleck's high window onto the calm street of Wenterglen's banking district.

"You can't?"

"I mean, I don't know if a little bit of magic, or a lot, is gonna come out, I don't want to give him a seizure or something."

"You mean that's not people getting possessed by your magic?"

"It's nothing that a witch can heal," she sighed. "This magic can bounce around in their brain for the rest of their lives, and it'd be my fault."

"You were just bluffing, huh," Relleck said, taking a stack of books from his desk and carefully arranging them on the bookshelf by the window. "You couldn't have killed that woman."

"Oh, I could've, but it would'na been on purpose." Y'Starren shrugged, standing up. "Look, I appreciate not having a bolt through my chest right now, but am I ever allowed a weekend off? Oh, and where's my money?"

"That wasn't discussed," Relleck said, not turning to face her. His finger trailed across the row of books, stirring a tiny

22

puff of dust that showed up in the sunlight shining in through the window. "But what could you possibly need? We give you everything here – food, shelter, clothes."

"A girl has needs," Y'Starren said, trailing her fingers through her hair as Relleck looked over his shoulder at her suspiciously. "Look at this braid. So empty. No decoration at all."

"Do they decorate their hair back in Seechatee?"

Y'Starren sighed pointedly. Seechatee was where she said she'd come from, a small farming town with locals that didn't "take too kindly to strangers."

"Fine," Relleck said. "I'll tell the steward to give you your pay at the end of each week."

"Cool," Y'Starren said, turning to go.

"In exchange for you practicing," Relleck said. "Learn to control what your magic does, at least."

***

The job at the Investigators' Guild was a high-paying, life-risking career where you were about at the end of your rope when you got to the middle of a job, Y'Starren had been told.

But you wouldn't think so to see her walking down the trail through the barbarian wilderness north of the Baneon wall, swinging a shortsword at the nearby bushes along the trail, training her ears for the sound of a river to follow. They were on their way to attempt, for the third time, to open communications with Chaza, the closed-off, technologically advanced country to the north of the barbarian wilderness. The only man that had ever come back alive from this mission was Merreth, and Relleck said that he hoped this time Y'Starren would come back with him. He'd told her she was the most powerful Gifted that had ever joined the Investigators' Guild. Yay for her.

"I can prove that I didn't do it," Merreth said for the third time.

"And yet, you refrain from actually doing so," Y'Starren sighed. "You afraid I'm going to murder you in your sleep?"

Merreth shot her a look as he slowed down behind her again. He lagged back a lot, keeping a full six feet away from her, at least, at all times.

"I'm not a murderer," Y'Starren looked back at him. "Though I might make an exception for you."

"I just happened to be there, Y'Starren," he insisted. "I had my sword out because I was afraid of you."

"You weren't afraid till I snapped my magic at you."

Merreth didn't answer as he tramped after her. Y'Starren had been raised in a small town with plenty of outlying farms and places to explore, so she was already used to forests. She was comfortable in the environment, but he apparently wasn't.

The morning mists had barely cleared before a heavy evening fog came down into the sunset-colored light ahead, gathering beneath the trees in a way that felt cozy and warm, as if to welcome them to sleep. Merreth had started to walk closer to her, eyes darting side to side with anxiety as they got closer.

"You know of the Warminds, don't you?" he asked.

She squinted at him. "I know nothing more than what you told me."

"But you grew up in Seechatee," he said, not making eye contact.

"Yeah, Seechatee, where we don't take too kindly to strangers, and we definitely don't talk about them," she said. "Just tell me."

He shook his head and sighed, making a "this close" finger sign at her, and then shaking his head again instead of elaborating. He came closer and lowered his voice as he shyly approached her.

"I don't bite," she said.

"Shh," he said. "No unnecessary talking. The Warminds will either kill us right away, or sacrifice us, if they find us."

She frowned. This was old news. Everyone knew that barbarians were like that.

"This tribe is brutal. Don't you get that?" Merreth said, more softly.

"So we avoid them?"

"We're in their territory, and this path isn't exactly new," Merreth said. "I'd have gone another way, but I don't ... know one."

Y'Starren walked thoughtfully forward, digesting the information. She was half-tempted to tease and pretend not to believe him, but she was starting to feel the need for some companionship. As they trekked up toward the top of a hill, she could see the last golden bits of sunset seeping through the murky fog.

"Does that look a little … " Merreth interrupted himself by sniffing, catching her arm suddenly to stop her. "I smell smoke."

She smelled smoke too. Merreth looked sick with panic.

"If they know we're here, it's too late," he muttered.

"Hie daen!" came a sudden yell from the side of the path.

Y'Starren flinched back from it, only to hear the same cry from the other side.

As she and Merreth backed away slowly, four archers rose out of the bushes, longbows bent and trained on the two of them.

"Ah, fuck," Merreth said.

"Stop," boomed a young man.

As he came down the path, eyes fixed on them, his feet took each step with a surety that said he knew every rock on the road. He was bald, and wore a crisscrossing, knotted network of strings across the top of his chest and shoulders, and a kilt of some kind on his lower half. His feet were booted in soft leather.

The two of them had stopped, and Y'Starren realized Merreth had stepped slightly behind her.

"So this is how you came back alive," she said. "By using the other investigators as shields."

"Just do your thing and get us out of here."

"Yeah, I'll use my Kill Touch from fifteen feet away."

The young man had brown eyebrows and eyes, and he was staring Y'Starren down from a height of about two inches taller.

"What are two witchlings doing in my forest?" he growled, stepping down the hill toward them.

"He speaks our language. Thank horizons," Merreth muttered.

The barbarian came to a stop a couple feet away from Y'Starren, hand on the hilt of a dagger on his hip. She flexed her fingers into a fist. She wasn't going to hurt him if she didn't have to.

"I guess I came directly to meet you and enchant you with my witchy skills," Y'Starren said.

That seemed too long and complicated for him to understand, because he frowned at her disgustedly.

"Maybe I should just kill you – " he started.

"No, no!" Merreth said, pushing past Y'Starren to face the barbarian, bowing repeatedly. Even Banes didn't really bow anymore. "We're just passing through. Just passing through. I promise."

"Yet if I said we were passing through one of your farms, you would kill me," he said. His eyes took on a grave, resentful expression.

"Well, that's different – " Merreth started, and the man slapped him.

Merreth bellowed in anger and hauled off with a punch at the man, who dodged up and back, drawing his knife quickly in the same motion.

"Get 'em, Y'Starren!" Merreth shouted.

The barbarian yelled something at the archers, who approached but did not shoot, appearing to be ready to do so. At the same time, Y'Starren heard a rustling and crunching through the underbrush behind them – someone had gone to get more of the barbarians, and the backup was almost there.

The leader stepped toward her.

"Come with us, and we will not hurt you." He reached for her sword with his left hand, holding a knife pointed downward in his right fist.

She stepped back and made a fair attempt at swinging the sword before he hooked her at the wrist with his knife as he redirected her swing, grabbed her hand, then stabbed the knife into her forearm.

She screamed and let go, clutching her arm at the wrist. He grabbed her by the hair, forcing her to bend over and dragging her up toward the other barbarians. Stomping into the brush underfoot to brace herself, she clutched the corded muscles of his bare calf. Then she pressed magic through his leg, forcing it to arc between her ring finger and thumb.

He fell with an anguished cry to his knees. Then something hit her in the back of the head and she fell face-first into moss and bark dust.

28

***

Y'Starren struggled toward the waning light as she heard them all around her, someone dragging her by one wrist, someone else dragging her by the other. The young man, apparently not too harmed, kicked her, cursing something in their wild dialect.

"Haela maeglegh!" He shouted.

She stumbled forward onto her feet. Her right arm, extended as she was dragged forward, was killing her. Every jerk felt like a rip of the mangled muscles. She gasped and bit the inside of her cheek, then cursed through her teeth.

"Blazing fuck." She sparked a shock through her left wrist and the barbarian let go.

She scrambled to the side, and the barbarian holding her other arm yanked her off her feet again and kicked her in the head and the ribs. Y'Starren knew from experience that it was nearly impossible to properly channel magic through an injury, and this was no different. The injured wrist remained securely in the barbarian's grasp as kicks, and now blows from sticks and hilts, were rained down on her back and protecting arm.

A panicked cry burst out from her as a hilt came down on her shoulder blade so hard it could've cracked it. The pain fucked with her magical control and it arced over her body, but she couldn't send it out into her attackers.

The barbarian leader's voice raised into a higher-pitched sound as he gave orders to the others. Y'Starren fell forward onto her elbows as she saw him aiming another kick at her. Protecting her head and face with her arms, she crouched down on her knees and shouted.

"Blazes – stop! Stop!"

"Die well, witchling." He kicked her.

She grunted in pain but didn't respond, hoping desperately that they would take that as a sign of submission and stop for now. A whimper of pain broke from her as she felt the blows pause.

The one holding her wrist tightened her grip cruelly just under the wound, and Y'Starren flinched but didn't pull back.

"Don't hurt her," the barbarian leader said. "No hurt."

Y'Starren bit her tongue as the pain from being stabbed in the arm ached unbearably. Blood dripped up her elbow. She stayed still with her other arm up.

"No hurt, understand?" the leader said again.

"Huh." Y'Starren nodded, not looking up. She was embarrassed because she was nearly crying, and didn't want to show it. People said that barbarians never cried.

Another Warmind came toward her, raising an unstrung bow, but the barbarian stopped them with a couple words.

"A maeglegh agnae."

With ... whatever that was, they dragged her off to their camp.

Y'Starren had heard stories about people being kidnapped by barbarians in order to be sacrificed to their gods, but even though the people in the stories often had hands cut off or eyeballs gouged out, they were usually much too tough to do anything more than grunt. Because of this, she had assumed that as injuries get worse, there's kind of a plateau of pain.

Either getting stabbed hadn't reached the plateau, or the whole thing was a myth in her mind, because Y'Starren was in so much pain from the cut in her arm that she couldn't even sit up.

She was writhing in front of the firepit in pain, clutching her left wrist just below the stab wound, gasping breaths in and then holding them so she didn't scream. They kicked her every time she screamed.

"Are you going to sacrifice us?" Merreth was saying quietly to the young barbarian, whose name was Eugh, which Y'Starren couldn't even pronounce in her mind.

"Not yet," Eugh said.

Y'Starren's knuckles were white as she gripped her wrist under the cut, trying desperately to focus her mind on anywhere else – anywhere else that wasn't in pain – as she felt heavy raindrops starting to sprinkle down between the trees.

At the sudden rain, the woman across the firepit from her cursed loudly, throwing down the tools she was using to try to start the fire in Y'Starren's direction. She stood up and walked around the firepit to Y'Starren, about to kick her.

"Molaidh," Eugh said. "Kicknae."

The girl – probably named Molaidh – stopped.

"Sorry … " Y'Starren said, almost half-sincerely. "It must be my fault it's raining."

"Witchlings are bad luck," Eugh said. "How's your arm?"

Y'Starren didn't answer for a moment, thinking he was mocking her, but when he didn't say anything more or even laugh, she lifted her head a bit to look at him. He was simply looking at her with a serious expression, waiting for a response.

She dropped her head.

"How do you think?" she said.

" … I don't understand," he said simply.

Another ache of pain made her writhe with her feet twisting together.

"It hurts, okay?" she said through her teeth. "When are you going to sacrifice us, anyway?"

"When the moon makes a circle, we'll kill you," he said, and she heard him moving toward her. "Don't hurt," he said.

She braced herself for another kick. When he put his hand on her upper arm, she flinched.

"You was holding a weapon in this hand," he said. "Sacrifices should be clean. You made me ruin you."

She clenched her teeth and waited for him to stop touching her before she released her breath. "Does this mean you're not going to sacrifice me?"

He shook his head.

"Maybe tonight I kill you, witchling."

"So we're just ... animals to you? Sacrifices?"

"We are barbarians to you," he said. "It's fair, isnae?"

It was true that she'd been raised to think of them as outsiders, as sun-cursed because they had no gifts. Back in Seechatee, a barbarian would've been killed on sight.

She closed her eyes and gritted her teeth against another shudder, images of her parents and of Wackee going off to the college alone blinking through her mind. Then the crazy fact that she was here, not even in her home country anymore, on the ground with a stab wound and about to be sacrificed "when the moon makes a circle." By barbarians.

Eugh was talking to the girl that had been failing to make a fire near Y'Starren's head, and when he knelt down again, he took her wounded arm and pulled it away from her body behind her back. She clenched her arm.

"Don't – " she started.

"Don't hurt," he said. "You're dirty."

He showed her a flask, which he then poured over the wound, washing away some of the dirt and dried blood. She took a deep breath and gritted her teeth, forcing herself not to pull away. It would be better to have it clean. And it would help it stop hurting.

"Now go," he said, pointing to a tree next to the one Merreth was tied to. They were going to tie her up next to him.

"Wait, I'm gonna – " she started, but he cut her off, drawing his dagger and nodding to the tree again.

"Go," he repeated.

Y'Starren hissed in frustration and showed him her fingers, at which he jumped to his feet, dagger ready.

"I'm not hurting you!" she said, putting her hand over the firepit. "I don't hurt. Watch."

As the barbarians closed in around her, leery of touching her but picking up their weapons, she picked up one of the charred chunks of wood from the last fire. She'd used small sticks to practice running her magic through at one exact point, and they all did the same thing – they smoked, sparked, and charred.

The barbarians had now closed in around her.

"I help. I'm helping!" she said, clenching the stick in her fist and forcing, willing the magic through it. At first it was just the surface that sparked and crackled, but soon the thing was snapping, hot and smoking in her fingers. She kept having to move her fingers in order to avoid being outright burned as the magic became fire.

"Ouch … " She hissed and dropped it into a nest of coals, then bent down to blow into the fire, and all her braids started falling down from behind her head where she'd tied them that morning. Clutching them all in her left hand and kneeling awkwardly over the pit, she bent down and blew on the fire, occasionally leaning back on her heels and imbuing it with a bit more spark from her left hand.

Finally, the damp tinder began to blaze up more reliably.

"There, see?" she said, wiping sweat off her forehead with a sooty hand, relieved as she realized they had relaxed a little.

"Witchling ... " someone muttered.

"Yeah, a witchling that saved your ass from a cold night. You're welcome." Y'Starren had almost forgotten about the wound. She smiled.

"Good witchling," Eugh said. "Now go."

***

Y'Starren leaned back against the sapling she'd been tied to – not the kind of sapling you can twist apart with your hands, but the kind that's about three inches through the trunk – watching the others cook and sit comfortably around the fire.

Eugh stood up from the fire with a long piece of meat stuck to his stick and walked toward Y'Starren. He jabbed the stick toward her face and she cursed, flinching back.

"Eat this," he said.

"Oh," she said. "Okay."

She tilted her head and grabbed the meat in her teeth, biting down hard as he jerked the stick away.

"Thank you," she said around the meat in her mouth. It was hot and crispy, but not too hot.

Eugh turned away.

"Wait – what about me?" Merreth interjected. "Am I getting some?"

"This good witchling started the fire." Eugh pointed his stick at Y'Starren. "*You* just complain." He turned away again as Merreth cursed at him.

"Fucking three days of this shit ... " Merreth said. "You should've killed them when I told you."

"As if I didn't try," Y'Starren said.

"Ai! Speaknae!" Molaidh made a throat-cutting gesture.

Merreth gave Y'Starren a withering look. He appeared to think very poorly of her at this point. She sighed and leaned her head back against the tree, squinting eyes reconnoitering the stars through the tips of the trees as if that was going to give her a strategic advantage.

All she wanted to do was focus on the mission. Focus on the money that was going to pay for Wackee's school and keep him safe, so the two of them, at least, could survive in a world that was meant to destroy them before they could destroy it.

I was made to break things.

It was a thought that recurred every time something like this happened. Before her, their parents had managed alright. But when she was born, they had to try to hide out even further from civilization, now that they had a crying baby to conceal.

She couldn't tell herself that she didn't blame her parents a little for choosing to have Wackee next. But she'd never blame him for something he couldn't help. Then came that morning that had ruined everything and gotten her here.

After that three months of school was up, Wackee would be found out and eliminated. A twelve-year-old couldn't be an investigator, no matter how well he bluffed – he'd be useless to the government.

The poor kid must feel so lonely right now ... if he was even okay.

No matter how much she tried to focus on the pain in her arm, or even just the feeling of missing her little brother, all she could think about was a mental zoom-in on the gash in her mother's neck, the feeling of her father's clay-like skin as he lay on his stomach on the stone. A bubble of grief welled up in her chest and her shoulders shook painfully as she began to sob softly, mind reeling blindly as she saw the horrible images over, and over, and over.

It was all over so fast. That morning, that wonderful morning, where her only problem had been the mild insult of having been left behind from some family adventure – what an adventure it was.

She moaned and bit her tongue to try to keep from letting anything else out.

"You're such a baby about this." Merreth scowled. One of the barbarians responded to him by hawking a well-deserved loogie in his direction.

Y'Starren wanted to beg him to tell her the truth, tell her what really happened. Because she kind of knew, but she couldn't let it go unless he admitted to it. What if he was telling the truth, and their real killer was somewhere out there, stalking Wackee and her?

She looked at Merreth, wisps of hair sticking to her tear-streaked face, unable to hide the rage and grief she felt toward him.

He rolled his eyes.

"You suncursed bastard," she swore under her breath.

"Suncursed" was a way to insult anyone who didn't have the orange hair and eyes or the gold-bronze skin tone of a "true" Bane. And he knew it. He set his face into a genuine grimace as he looked away.

It was just as the Warminds were lying down to sleep when there was a sudden shout, and then a scream.

"Naimheaden!" came the cry from the sentries as they rushed back up the slope toward the camp. The tribe began to scramble to their feet, grabbing knives, axes, sticks, and bows from where they'd set them as they lay down to sleep.

Women clutched their babies to their chests, wrapping them in the narrow cloths that everyone here wore instead of hoods, and their children sprang to their defense with their own crude weapons. Everyone was shouting and screaming, and their enemies were surrounding them with torches that gleamed through the trees all around in tiny points of light.

Merreth was hissing at her. "Y'Starren. Hey. Dumbshit."

She glared at him. "Yes, suncursed?"

"Get us out of here!"

"And what exactly do you expect me to do when I'm tied up like this?"

"I can feel it," he said. Y'Starren realized he had pressed his palm into the pine needle bed behind him. He was a Seer, which meant he could extend his consciousness into whatever he was touching. "Their feet on the needles. There are over five hundred."

Y'Starren's mouth opened. Five hundred was more barbarians than she had ever imagined together in the wild lands.

"Someone's going to drop a knife behind you," he said. "Get so your feet are pointed the other way, so you can pick it up with your feet. Then cut us free."

Y'Starren reluctantly did as he said, groaning with annoyance and some pain from her wounds. She didn't ask him how he knew what was going to happen – he was a Clairvoyant Seer; you don't ask Clairvoyants how they know. They can't ever tell you, but they're usually right anyways.

"And don't you dare leave me here," he added. "You need me."

"Don't worry," Y'Starren grunted as she maneuvered herself into the brush behind her at the base of the tree. "You are *top* of my priority list."

She was pretty sure she was now halfway on top of a termite nest, because she could feel little itchy, crawly sensations going down her buttcrack.

The camp was being overrun, and it happened in the space of less than a minute. A couple arrows clattered into the brush around them, but for the most part, the other tribe came in waving torches and battering the Warminds over the head with them, flaming tar and ripped cotton bits flying from the torches into the damp underbrush and smoking out into cinders.

"Who are they?" Y'Starren shouted, since Merreth seemed to know so much about barbarians.

"Also Warminds," he shouted back.

"How can you tell?"

"Bald!" he shouted over the screaming, which was coming from both sides.

They were, in fact, all bald, she realized. Even the women and children.

The invaders got even louder as they began to spear and stomp the Warminds that had captured the two Banes.

Then it happened – a knife slipped from the belt of one of the invaders and landed by Y'Starren's feet. She stuck out her bare feet in the direction of the blade, which was slightly crooked. It was an ugly iron thing, with only the edge sharpened and metal slivers rolled at the base of the blade, but she pulled it close with her feet and maneuvered herself around so that her hands could reach it.

"You've got about forty-five seconds before they notice us, Y'Starren!" Merreth shouted, just audible above the other shouting.

Y'Starren muttered, "Not helping!" as she ripped the clumsy thing against the twisted plant cord that had bound her hands. She was accustomed to that kind of twine, otherwise she would've been shocked at its natural strength. However, she wore lengths of cord around her body, as part of her decorations and bracelets and armbands and such, so she knew that this cord could hold her body weight easily if required. The knife sawed through and she wiggled her wrists free of the last strands. She crawled to Merreth, cutting at the cord across the tree rather than freeing his hands directly. He'd have to wiggle them apart on the way – there was no time.

"But I need my sword. I need my sword," he was insisting. Perhaps he Clairvoyantly knew he'd need it. But she had no time for the delicate task of trying not to cut his hands as she ripped through the twine, and if they only had forty-five seconds, that time was up.

He barely ducked out of the way of a sword slash aimed at his head, and they fled.

"They put up a perimeter," he grunted to her as they knelt in the underbrush fifteen feet away. "I can feel their feet there and there." He pointed. The tribe members were trying to escape the slaughter, but the invading Warminds were catching them as they fled.

"Here," he said, pointing as a woman with a baby raced forward through the trees. "They'll probably get caught. We'll use them as a decoy."

Y'Starren watched in horror as another barbarian ambushed the woman, springing out of the bushes and running her through with a narrow, iron-tipped spear, which was illuminated by the crazed, waving torch of the other Warminds behind Y'Starren and Merreth. She heard the baby whimper as it fell from her arms.

Merreth grabbed Y'Starren by the hair and yanked her to her feet. They fled.

Even after they ran past the perimeter that the barbarians had created, Merreth continued to pull her forward, though he caught her by the wrist when she lifted his hand from her hair. A glance at his panicked face told her everything she needed to know – they weren't safe yet.

"I can feel them," he said, pausing as he twisted his foot into the clay underneath the pine needles, probably sensing them. "They're coming."

Then he yanked her onward.

Y'Starren's lungs burned as she followed him, determined not to be outlasted, determined to escape, even though she felt like she was going to collapse.

Do it for Wackee, she told herself. *Get that money for him. Keep him safe at the college. Do it for him.*

Finally, Merreth pulled her up toward a rocky outcropping, where she nearly bumped her head into the stone jutting out over them as she slumped down with him. Her chest ached and her lungs burned.

"Now stay quiet," Merreth panted.

She sank back into the bushes against the cold stone, and in a matter of minutes, her dizzy head relaxed and her eyes closed. She fell asleep.

***

Merreth was physically kicking himself as they trudged up the mountainside. There was a goat path lightly trod into the side of the steep hill, which they managed to stick to with only a few slips here and there. It didn't help that Merreth was scuffing the back of his left calf with his right foot here and there, cursing at himself.

"Should've been blazing paying attention. Don't know why I took the blazing path. Stupid. Stupid."

"Didn't you say it's going to be dangerous no matter what path we take?" Y'Starren called back to him.

He fell silent for a while.

"So what exactly are we doing?" Y'Starren said. "When we get to Chaza?"

She was, as they walked, scanning the trees for bears. They were so big and contrasted so clearly with the greenery that you'd think you'd see them right away. But Y'Starren had seen several bears, and they were always suddenly just there. It was terrifying every time.

" ... Delegation," Merreth replied after a very long pause.

Y'Starren stopped and looked back at him, licking her lips. She was thirsty as fuck and they still hadn't reached the river, though she could hear it far ahead and below.

"You're just saying a long word because you don't want to explain," Y'Starren said.

"What are you stopping for?" he said impatiently, having caught up.

"Tell me what we're doing in Chaza," she said irritably.

"I said, we're doing delegation." He scowled. "You're getting your money either way. Now get going, I'm getting thirsty."

The hillside was rocky and difficult, and every few minutes Y'Starren would think again about stopping and resting. Merreth insisted on going on the side of the cliff where it would be harder for people to group up around them, with better visibility, and he also insisted on hurrying. No breaks. It was terribly frustrating, even though deep down she knew she would've agreed if he'd given her the choice. The walk should've taken them ten days, but he was trying to get them through it in three.

It was getting dark by the time they finally started traveling down toward the river they'd been hearing. It was still so far away.

Mist lowered around them once more as their bare feet clutched the slope on the way down. The river got louder and louder, till it seemed like they must be reaching rapids. Maybe her ears had just gotten accustomed to the quietness of nature, though, because it was just a stream, ten or twenty feet across.

Though the Banes tended to boil or filter their water to prevent curses, Y'Starren couldn't stop herself from plunging her hot, dirty feet in and scooping up a handful to drink immediately.

"You fool," Merreth shouted above the sound of the water. "Just get some in your flask to boil."

Y'Starren did, but she hardly cared about any curses at the moment. The water was sweet and tasted rocky and fresh, just like the mountain moss smelled. It was freezing cold on her bare feet, which was a welcome change from the heat and dust and bruises from the day's long climb.

Despite the pain and the sweat and her wounded arm, she was charmed by the magic around them. Even the birds seemed excited to see them, not alarmed or anything. Blue dusk melted down in the gap between the trees that the canyon river formed, making the faraway landscape look like the ghosts of trees and shadows. Somehow, despite the absence of people, there was still a vibrant amount of magic in the air for her to gather in her body.

"Let's go up a bit further, make a fire," Merreth called.

Y'Starren realized she had just been standing in the water with her wet hands on her hips, staring around herself happily. When he spoke, she was reminded of a few very bitter things she didn't want to think about. Her shoulders slumped a little and she sighed.

"I found some tea leaves," Merreth added.

She perked up again and turned to smile at him.

"Oh, good!" she said. "Let's have a proper Bane dinner."

***

It was darker now. Trees loomed black against the sky around them as Y'Starren and Merreth huddled in their cloaks by the small cooking fire, sipping some admittedly well-made tea from their flasks.

"So, tell me about yourself," Merreth said. "All you've done is complain all day. Cheer us up for a change."

"So you want me to tell you about my dead family to cheer you up?" she said sourly. Her voice was raised just above the crackle of the fire. They were terrified that someone nearby would see it, but they were about at the edge of the Grass People's territory, Merreth said. Tomorrow's walk would be much safer.

"I'm just curious." Merreth shrugged, starting to lean back, then getting annoyed that there was no chair-back for him out in the wilderness. He grunted and shuffled around, finally leaning forward again and putting his chin in his hands.

His forty-year-old wrinkled face was always a bit irritable-looking, but tonight, it looked a little more alive. Maybe he'd missed the wild woods. Y'Starren had never seen any landscape as beautiful.

"Well, my mother was the smartest woman I ever met," she said. "Pure sarcasm, this woman. She acted like she hated everyone, but she was extremely kind."

Merreth eyed her judgmentally. "Go on."

"I'm loving the encouragement." Y'Starren rolled her eyes, but she settled back on her bundle of extra clothes, crossing her legs and taking another awkward gulp of tea. "And Father was a paranoid, superstitious woodsman. Powerful, strong."

She paused. She was not going to tell him about her brother.

"Was he a good guy?" Merreth asked, staring down into the coals now. He looked a little more bitter and a little more thoughtful than normal.

Y'Starren realized she couldn't answer. She couldn't tell him that her father was the most handsome, excitable guy she'd ever witnessed chase a squirrel. She couldn't even bear to think about the play fights they used to have, that day with the apples, because now each old memory of him was matched with the picture of her father on his stomach. The hard, cold skin on his neck.

She grimaced and looked up into the sky, blinking back tears. She couldn't cry in front of this guy. Not while she thought what she thought of him – just in case this man really was the fucking killer.

"What do ya know, it's bedtime," she said, voice breaking slightly.

She pulled her cloak up closer around her shoulders, wrapped her feet up in a spare woolen tunic, and lay back on the pile of soft branches and leaves she'd collected to sleep on while they were making camp. She blinked at the haze of fog that drifted over their hillside camp, built on a small plateau, where Merreth could look down the hill from his seat across from her. To his credit, he'd given her the safer place to sleep. It was probably just a strategic choice, since he was the Clairvoyant.

"Hey, I'm ... " he said slowly. "I'm sorry."

***

Two days later, Y'Starren followed closely behind Merreth as he guided her through the forest toward a massive industrial building that was somehow embedded in the cliff. They could only occasionally make it out in the distance, but Merreth said that that was the facility they were trying to reach. It was some kind of laboratory, he said, and that was where he met with the Chazans for private government deals.

The Chazans, called Ghost Men by the superstitious, were said to be somewhat small and squat, dark but also pale, and freakishly intelligent. They were said to be able to wave their hand and kill you. They could also fly. Then again, none of the people Y'Starren spoke to had ever actually seen one.

Y'Starren figured she should give them a chance to be less frightening than the legends claimed.

As they walked, she found herself gingerly avoiding patches of gravel that seemed to have been intentionally carted in. Why would you bother to make a path out of something so uncomfortable to walk on? There was more and more gravel as they went forward.

Finally, they had to go off the path to step over some barbed wire, and then they crossed a ravine and reached a flight of steps.

"Is this sandstone?" Y'Starren said, bare feet spreading on the cool, gritty steps luxuriously after over a half-mile of gravel path.

"Cement," Merreth replied. "We're almost there."

"How 'almost' are we talking this time?" Y'Starren said. He'd said that same sentence three times already today and once yesterday, so she had no real frame of reference.

He pointed upward as the steps went up the hill, winding side to side to avoid drops and getting higher and higher.

49

She couldn't see it through the trees, but she assumed that the building was up there somewhere. Finally, as they reached the top of a hill where the steps crested, Y'Starren could see the building they were approaching – what looked like massive cubes of the purest dark crystal, gripped into the side of the jungle cliff like black knuckles, rising above even the tallest trees with about four levels of massive architecture.

Despite its apparent newness, the cement walkways were mossy and somewhat overgrown. As they got closer, it was clear that they had been swept.

Finally, they reached a modest-looking door with a teensy reinforced window. Merreth hesitated, glancing back at her, then knocked on the door.

There was no answer.

He raised a meaty fist and banged on the solid green door this time. Y'Starren heard it echoing down a hallway that sounded almost like a canyon. And finally, the sound of feet and voices, and the door opened all the way to reveal a man with black hair and a face so pale it was almost white.

The Ghost Men.

The Ghost Man looked over Merreth's shoulder.

"Is gifted?" he said.

"Well, you're one to get to the point, aren't you," Y'Starren smiled, holding out her hand.

The man barely looked at her, but nodded at Merreth and asked them to come inside, using an odd dialect that Y'Starren found she couldn't understand.

As the door closed behind her, Y'Starren noticed that men in white coats that didn't even look warm were crowding around them, eyeing the tall Bane, and writing in notepads when they looked at Y'Starren. She noticed only after a minute or so that the Chazans didn't touch each other much.

"Her gift?" he asked.

"I only speak to Mainmwim," Merreth said. "Get me Mainmwim."

"Lord Mainmwim is of industries!" the man protested. "Accords with Yeckswem, is much able."

Y'Starren squinted, trying her best to understand what they were saying. She didn't know what "industries" or "accords" meant, but the rest of the words were definitely Bane.

At that moment, a tall, scornful-looking Chazan with a long, lined face hurried up with a clipboard stuffed into one of the massive pockets in his lab coat.

"Yeckswem." The man that had opened the door bowed and moved out of the newcomer's way. "Yeckswem is of accords. I am of industries, my apologies – "

He broke off as Yeckswem put a hand on his shoulder.

"Winwyn, stop," he said, and then he turned a pair of hard, clever eyes on Y'Starren and fished around in his pocket for something.

He pulled out a black box-shaped thing, then suddenly jabbed it into Y'Starren's arm. The jab was hard enough to bruise, and at the same time there was a powerful jolt of magic, which repeated mechanically. She was too shocked to react for a moment, taking in the energy quickly and feeling it spark in her fingertips, like it did when she needed to touch the ground pretty soon. The wax-like floor was almost bouncy, and it did not respond at all when she tried to push her excess magic into it.

"Uh – hey. Stop," she said, pulling away. It had left two bruised marks on her arm. "That kind of hurts!"

Yeckswem was staring at the box and shaking it and adjusting knobs on it with a panicked expression.

"I'm so sorry," Merreth started stammering. "She's not – I didn't know she could – "

Yeckswem glared at Merreth as someone screamed "Security!" and all the scientists scrambled away from Y'Starren like she was going to bite them.

"This subject is defective," Yeckswem was growling at Merreth.

"Excuse me?" Y'Starren said. "I'm the defective one here?"

And then it hit her.

Something slammed into her from the left just behind her and knocked her sideways, and before she realized what was happening, people had jumped in – people in gray and yellow bodysuits with masks over their faces – solid black masks like crystal – and she was struggling to get out of their grip, grunting and now biting. And her magic was sparking and arcing out, zapping their hands, and then they'd grab another part of her body.

This time, she wasn't letting them kidnap her. She'd seen where that would go – she could get killed.

Sticks battered and rebounded off her back and arm as she struggled toward the door, lunging at the one scientist who blocked the way with his short arms spread out as if to stop her. She smashed a fist into his face, and then pushed magic out of her fist and into his broken nose, and he clutched his face and fell to the ground, seizing and making choking noises. She put her hand on the door and could immediately tell it was metal from the way it accepted the energy in her body.

Involuntarily the magic started to jump into the door, and she willed it back into herself and twisted the knob.

But suddenly she was yanked back by an arm around her neck. It was tight and thick. She couldn't breathe or think. Her face went puffy as she fought against his grip.

She batted behind herself with her bare hand, searching for skin – the easiest thing to hurt with her magic. All she found was a tacky, waxy material that was somehow completely blocking her magic just as effectively as the floor was. Her legs were kicking reflexively, and it wasn't helping. He just wouldn't let her breathe.

"Get it! Get it!" people were encouraging him.

They dragged her backward, so weak now that she could hardly move, and tears were running from the corners of her eyes.

The last thing she saw was Merreth, calmly watching them go with that serious, almost blank expression he so often wore.

He'd betrayed her.

Her vision went black as she felt something jab into her arm.

***

Y'Starren lay limp on the floor as her eyelids fluttered open. The floor was completely free of any kind of smell, but her body was all twisted up in an awkward pose, like she'd just been dropped there. She trembled, trying to move, but every part of her felt like it was strapped down with weights, even though she couldn't feel or see anything besides her own body. She flopped awkwardly, head dragging on the ground as she braced herself on a shaking elbow, shoulder poking up as she tried to get the rest of herself up. Her hair draped forward, strands of it trailing into her eyes, and her braids made a jagged curtain around the corners of her vision. Her string bracelets and anklets were only a small comfort – she could barely feel them. She always used them as a sort of grounding technique for anxiety when she was worried about getting found by the government.

As she struggled and failed to rise on the floor, she heard their shoes around her, talking about her, though she mostly couldn't understand what they were saying. She gathered that they had intentionally made her this weak, that they were waiting for Mainmwim, and they were trying to figure out how to "ground" her. They acted like she was some kind of problem they'd never had to deal with before – as if they couldn't have just not kidnapped her.

"Is a gifted?" a new voice came in. A door closed. The room was small and had muffling walls, so their voices sounded personal, intimate.

"Lord Mainmwim." Their voices were more hushed than normal. "Subject does not engage properly with G-H-B. Is gifted of electrical charges."

A small silence fell as a pair of black shoes approached. Y'Starren lifted her heavy head to see the bottom of his white slacks.

"Like a charger ... " Mainmwim knelt down in front of her and took her under the chin, tilting her head back to see her face. "Charger," he said, "why have you stopped charging the scientists?"

"Is it just me," Y'Starren slurred, "or are you suddenly talkin' right?"

"Bane dialect is not right," Mainmwim said, still scanning her with his eyes. "So, why have you stopped charging the scientists?"

Y'Starren trembled in the effort to speak and keep from collapsing.

"He left me here, didn't he ... " she said.

"A simple matter of money," Mainmwim said. "Now I've answered two of your questions. Answer mine, or this exchange will not be so kind."

Y'Starren dropped her weight, exhausted, forehead on the ground as she struggled to speak.

"I ran out of charge, okay?" she said. "I can't believe they just sold me out like this. I'm gonna kill them ... "

"And how do you get more charge?" Mainmwim said.

"Ask Yeckswem," Y'Starren said, thinking of his little box of magic. If they wanted magic, why didn't they just ask him?

There was a pause as the two of them communicated something with a shrug and a point.

"Yeckswem will torture you if you do not answer," Mainmwim said after a moment.

" ... I don't understand ... " Y'Starren said, breath huffing against the ground. "I don't understand! What's happening? Why are you threatening me? You drugged me!"

"He will torture you," Mainmwim repeated.

"Well, isn't that quaint!" Y'Starren's voice trembled. "Why? What did I ever do to you?"

There was a sigh as people shuffled around her, and the door opened and closed again.

"Yeckswem is going to get something to hurt you," Main-mwim said. "Now answer the question, or else."

She was shaking, trying to process exactly what was happening. She had to give him some kind of answer, but she could hardly think.

"I get more ... charge ... over time," she said. "I – I don't know much about it myself."

She couldn't tell them everything. She didn't want them to know what she could do. It was going to be a surprise. Yeah, a surprise. That helped a little. She smiled grimly, face hidden by the floor and the fallen braids, which still smelled like forest and smoke. Quite the surprise it would be.

"You said to ask Yeckswem," Mainmwim said, sounding irritated. "So you know you are using electricity. What I'm asking you is how you gather it."

"Ughhh ... " she groaned. She could feel a little bit of her strength coming back very gradually, and she raised up on her other elbow, lifting her head just enough to glare at Mainmwim from under her eyebrows. "I collect the magic over time, and then I push it out of my hands." She wouldn't tell them that she could also push it out of any other place in her body with a little more effort. "How is that not enough for you? We don't have 'chargers' back where I'm from. I'm the only one," she lied again. "I barely know how my gift works myself."

The door opened and closed again, and someone else knelt next to her – Yeckswem. Suddenly there was a pinching sensation on her neck, and then an intensifying burn as the flesh on her neck was pinched and twisted in a set of pliers.

She winced and tried to push him away. She tried to send a shock of magic through the metal pliers, but it didn't reach him, and her skin began to burn.

"Stop – stop!" she gasped, flopping a limp arm out to try to grab Yeckswem's hand. He shifted the angle, twisting more. She whimpered in pain, lip quivering as her eyes watered. "It hurts ... please ... "

"Then answer the question." Mainmwim's voice came from up above her, completely detached. "How do you gather charge?"

Yeckswem let go of the piece of flesh, and as the blood flowed back into it, it burned even worse. She groaned and ducked in to cover her neck. He moved the pliers about an inch down from the last place and she felt the cold clamps begin to squeeze.

"Wait – wait!" she gasped. "I don't know, I swear."

He twisted and pinched till she screamed, cringing in to try to protect her shoulder. She wasn't going to tell them shit. She was going to figure out how to make the Kill Touch really kill everyone she touched, and she was going to get the hell out and make Wackee safe.

She cursed and panted as he released the chunk of skin, shuddering a little. She collapsed inward, covering the bruises with her right hand, breaths puffing against the waxy floor.

"Please just let me go," her voice creaked.

"Behends not," Winwyn said from behind Yeckswem. "Accords?"

"Withal – " Yeckswem started.

"Is fascinating," Mainmwim interrupted.

Winwyn stepped up beside Yeckswem, and Y'Starren, who was watching them in her periphery, noticed a slightly disturbed expression on his face as he glanced at her.

"Haply is instinct," he said softly. "Tolerates the tase, yet it behends little. Haply we test of it?"

Somehow, their dialect was actually starting to make a little sense, though it was annoying. Or maybe she just didn't like the speakers.

"Accords," Mainmwim said, and the scientists left Y'Starren alone for a while in the room, probably watching her through the massive dark windows on one side of the room.

After a while, a few of them came back with Yeckswem and helped him drag her away.

She was dumped into a room on a cot-like bed, where the ceiling was lined with lights, and the door had one of those tiny windows.

White, fragile chairs and tables crowded the corner of her vision, and as the door closed, she saw the orange heads of two other Banes. She felt her chest sinking into the bed, making it hard to breathe.

The Banes' tan faces were a welcome sight. There was a blue-eyed man in his forties, hair going white and a wandering expression. He introduced himself as Nomad.

The other was a young boy named Len. He had a beautiful face that reminded her a little bit of Wackee, though his hair lay flat and dull against his head instead of spiky and vibrant like her brother's. He looked gentle, but frightened.

She looked around the room, with its white, noise-canceling paneled walls, the sound of some kind of construction in the next room, with the off-and-on massive whirring of machinery. The tables in this room had some food set out on them in strange shiny black trays. There was also a chess set. Len was shyly, secretively touching one of her braids. The two other prisoners had their hair cropped very short into a perfectly even cut that looked like it had been shaved by an expert barber. That seemed unlikely, but perhaps these advanced Chazans had some sort of machinery that made it easy.

"So, Merreth has just been selling the other investigators, huh?" Y'Starren said. It was getting easier to speak, though her chest was still heavy and her limbs were practically immobile.

"I don't know about him," Nomad said. "I was a Teleporter, but ... I can't seem to do it anymore. Not after the ... "

"Come on, I don't have all day," Y'Starren said.

Nomad smiled slightly.

"It's so good seeing a fresh face after all these years," he sighed. "You're about the age my daughter would be now ... "

For a moment, his eyes clouded with tears, and he rubbed his hand over his stubble repeatedly like he was trying not to cry.

Y'Starren's heart began to sink. Years? And that bit about his daughter ...

"I'll tell you one thing, Y'Starren," Nomad said. "Don't ... try anything."

As he spoke, he rubbed a deep red scar across his neck under his ear.

"Look, Nomad, you take your own advice, because someone's gotta," Y'Starren said. "And it's not gonna be me."

Nomad looked away with a resentful grimace.

"Of course you'd be like that," he said. After a silent pause, he added, "I mean, you've seen what they'll do to you. Suncursed bastards already hurt you." Y'Starren saw him turn his face away to rub roughly at his eyes. "Can't you just call it enough and cooperate?"

She sighed and closed her eyes.

"No," she said. "I have a brother to protect."

Nomad shook his head. "Nothing's worth what they'll do to you."

Y'Starren shivered.

"Ooh, sounds exciting," she said. "Now I'm gonna sleep. Wait – " She opened one eye and squinted at Nomad. "Are they gonna come back for me, do you think?"

"It's okay," Len said again. "They'll probably wait for the drug to wear off. They like us conscious and able to feel everything for their ... tests."

He shuddered.

Y'Starren sighed and settled back, imagining a canopy of trees, black against the cold night sky.

"They never turn the lights off," was the last thing she heard before she fell asleep to Nomad's hollow, droning voice.

***

As she was led out between the guards, Y'Starren mentally mapped out the place. She focused on her magic moving through her body, finding her fingers snapping with it. After the box, which was apparently called a taser, she had become rich with magic and had gathered a little from the air.

If she could figure out her gift faster than they could, she'd have the edge on that. Then all she'd need to know was the layout.

It seemed simple. She bit the inside of her cheek as she looked around, mentally rehearsing the layout as she walked. Things were never simple when they seemed simple, but she was going to make it happen anyway.

There was a chair made of panels in a tiled room with a black ceiling, and there were massive bright lamps shining down onto the chair. She noticed restraints by the head, arms, and leg areas, and shivered.

They passed by huge, bright panels full of letters, numbers, and a few images that made no sense to her, on the way to the panel chair. Except for one – it had a gridwork of what must absolutely be man-made paths. She knew it was, because it said "map" on top. These Chazans probably assumed she couldn't even read. They'd been treating her like she would've treated a barbarian.

"Go!" The guard punched her in the back impatiently. "Sit!"

Y'Starren whirled around, about to punch him, and reeled back the response just in time, biting her cheek and stepping backward while lowering her eyes meekly.

"Thought better of it?" the guard said.

"Oh, I'm not one to talk back to my betters," Y'Starren scoffed, not looking up.

"Repeat it," the guard said.

Y'Starren didn't, but the scientists were now flooding into the room, many of them staring at her with a piercing kind of interest that made her feel like an animal.

"Sit," the guard huffed, pointing at the chair.

Her stomach ground with anxiety as she did, panels wobbling slightly under her weight. Despite a lifetime of fending off starvation, she'd become pretty well-built and heavy and tall for her family, which was barely above average for a Bane.

They started fastening her wrists and ankles in the restraints immediately – except for her left hand.

"Is what?" someone said, brushing some of her stray hair away from her arm and pointing to the wound. "Is a wound, but how came it?"

"Never seen a cut before?" Y'Starren said.

The scientist – a short woman with the typical sharp eyes, hair pulled into a graceful half-ponytail – looked shocked that Y'Starren had dared to speak, much less say that.

"What, are your subjects usually tamer?" she sneered. "I was raised in the – "

A hand was clapped to her forehead and a thick leather strap came halfway over her eyes, and she grimaced as her head was pinned against the back of the chair.

Great. Now I look stupid.

"Tell me of it," the woman said. The other scientists had backed up a bit to wait for something anyway, and she was now the only one close to Y'Starren. She tapped above the wound, making Y'Starren wince. "Tell me of it. Behend me?"

" ... I behend it," Y'Starren grunted. "We came into the War-minds territory, and they must hate Banes as much as we hate them. I had a sword in this hand – " She flinched as the woman touched the wound. She realized the scientist was applying some kind of gel to it.

"The fuck is that?" Y'Starren said through gritted teeth.

"Tell it." The woman didn't look up.

Y'Starren turned her eyes back to the ceiling.

"Anyway, the leader of the barbarians stabbed me right there in the arm and made me drop my sword. It's probably still out there."

There was a pause, then there was a small applause from the gathered scientists and the two guards that had remained in the room.

"Affable, affable," they said, which must be some sort of praise.

"Stories are what Chazans like," the woman said slowly, clearly attempting to make herself easier for Y'Starren to understand.

The woman taped a bandage over the wound, and Y'Starren realized that the dull ache that had been there was slowly fading. She tried to look down at her arm, but couldn't move her head enough. The woman had just made it stop hurting somehow. Whether it was for some evil reason or not, Y'Starren was grateful, and the clenching in her throat released a little. She swallowed.

"Thank you," she said.

When Yeckswem came in with a sour expression, beady eyes fixed on Y'Starren, she felt naked once again. Her braids, thickened with ribbons from last week, itched at the back of her head as she watched him come up and start tapping buttons at a rapid pace into the computer he was standing at. She'd heard enough terms and enough new words of the Chazan dialect to begin piecing together a bit about the world where these people lived and conducted their experiments. The only thing that was bothering her was the difference between rubber and plastic – she couldn't figure it out.

He walked over to her, pulled over a tray on a stand which rattled with tools, and pulled something out of his pocket. Two things. The first, the black taser he'd tried to hurt her with yesterday, and the second, the pliers. Her bruised, torn neck burned already just from looking at them. He was giving her a look as he showed them to her.

It wasn't even a demand for compliance – no, those eyes said "I'm going to use these on you."

He pulled something from the tray which was connected to a cord. It was a pair of discs, which he taped to two of her fingers, her forefinger and her middle finger. His hands were cold and unpleasant.

"Charge this one, Charger." He tapped her forefinger. Many of the scientists had taken positions around the screens, looking, pointing, whispering observations. Had they been watching her in the room with the other prisoners? Creeps.

"Start," he said, irritated, already looking to the pliers, where Y'Starren's own eyes kept wandering. Maybe if she didn't give him an excuse ...

She closed her eyes, pretending to find it difficult, and trailed a miniscule amount of energy into her finger, which was sucked in greedily by the disc.

"How long are you going to keep me here?"

Yeckswem didn't answer, frowning at the readings.

"More," he said, tapping her hand.

Y'Starren wanted to shock him up through that finger he was tapping her with, but she forced herself not to. She didn't want to be hurt again.

She grunted and strained against the bonds, pretending to try to put more power into the finger, then reversed the flow and put it through the other one.

"Ah – it's just hard to control it," she said.

"This control – you did it to another," he said. He took the pliers.

"Wait, I – " Y'Starren struggled against her fear. She couldn't let them win. She needed to figure out her powers first. She'd never been much good at making tests, but she had to copy their tactics and try. And she had to buy time to figure it out faster than they did. They couldn't know the extent of her power.

She pushed another almost negligible amount of magic into the disc.

Suddenly a pinching pain seared into her arm as Yeckswem clamped the pliers down. She hissed a curse, wrist jerking at the restraint. Then she forced herself to focus away. They would not make her – then she realized that the power had reflexively surged out of her, as it often did when she was frightened or in pain. She was both right now, heart pounding and pain ripping up and down her arm.

"Horizons," she cursed hoarsely.

"Thought it," Yeckswem muttered, squeezing harder, twisting till the skin broke. She screamed through clamped-shut teeth. "More torture." Yeckswem snapped his fingers at one of the other scientists. "Penalty of pliers must of revise, Winwyn." Yeckswem tossed them onto the tray. "Encounter such an efficat, and keep such torture no mennus."

Gotta like the sound of "torture." The thought flashed through her head, but she didn't say it. She was focused on not letting out her magic. She attempted to constrain the tide to what had already been released, creating a plateau. She didn't want them to know just how much magic she could release.

"Line, haply?" Winwyn said, hurrying to a metal chest of drawers.

"Line, yeh." Yeckswem nodded.

Winwyn pulled something out of a drawer. It was a bundle of three thin metal sticks, wrapped at the base with wire that formed a handle. He handed it to Yeckswem.

"Behold, the line." Yeckswem showed it to her. Then he tapped her leg with it; it was cold, and even the light flick stung a little. "Charge the electrode as charged in the scientist you punched."

Charge it like you charged the guy you punched. Y'Starren understood, but –

Fwip – the line snapped into her forearm above the restraint and she gasped, body reflexively yanking at the restraints. It stung across her arm.

"Stop – " she whispered, and he brought it down again.

She whimpered through her teeth, twisting and tugging at the once-gentle restraints, which now seemed hard as rock around her wrists. Head pulled back like that, everyone could see her face contorting as he continued to whip her till the blood ran down her arm. She screamed. Her voice bounced off the plaster walls and ceiling and rattled the lamps. The chair shuddered under her jerking body as she held her breath and screamed again.

All the control she'd had was gone, and she was screaming in pain over and over, power pulsing out of her through the fingers of both hands and feet, scorching her skin black under each pulse of pain and magic after each lash to her arm. Then there was a snap, a faint acrid smoke, as the connection broke. She'd overloaded it.

"Output severed," one of the scientists commented. Y'Starren sobbed in agony, shuddering and heaving huge breaths. She didn't want them to know how much they were hurting her; she didn't want to let them know shit until she'd figured it out. She hadn't even really noticed that pain forced her to lose control of the magic that was always waiting to be released from her body.

She groaned, tears pouring down the sides of her face into her hair.

69

She felt the meager remains of her magic drifting down her chest toward the torn flesh of her arm, as it liked to do. It often collected around her injuries. She focused past the pain, closing her eyes and picturing herself in the woods. She used to take the energy from the air, very slowly, as she watched the clouds pass across the moon and stars, on nights when it was warm enough to lay outside on the blankets. The static from the blankets was a little disruptive to the magic collection process.

She made the magic spark across her fingers, keeping them close together so that no one else could see them. The lights that were shining down on her were so bright, but she kept her eyes closed, now imagining resting on the grass at midday, the day with the apples.

A sudden sob broke from her before she knew it. She grimaced and forced it back, pretending to be reacting to the pain with a weird little whimper. At least the awkwardness brought her thoughts away from that last good day.

"Yeckswem has the right," the female scientist from before commented. "Would that a shocking did such a trick."

"Hold – such is it!" Yeckswem snapped his fingers. "Output of it haply subcedes of the gen."

"Tending it," the scientist replied. "Of the cut and the back-up gen plan. Good good?"

Y'Starren sniffled. *Keep acting like your blazing language is valid*, she thought, biting her cheek and grimacing again. *I hate your blazing language.*

"Good, Menyth," Yeckswem said, pointing at two of the other scientists. "Accords."

They left the room, and the female scientist, apparently called Menyth, took out more of the ointment she'd used on Y'Starren's other arm with a sigh of resignation to attend to her new wounds. She was the first person to care for Y'Starren like that here in the facility. But Y'Starren didn't thank her again. The bitch just stood by while they tortured her. She was the same as the others.

***

Back in the room with the other prisoners, Y'Starren focused on drawing the electricity from one side of her body to another, charging her hand, her foot, her neck, but not releasing it. Each time, all it took was imagining Yeckswem's hand there to provoke a magical flow. Controlling herself enough to keep from sparking it off from there was a little harder, so she often had to pull it away and create a small rhythmic flow inside her.

She also practiced sending it into the metal bedframe, not retrieving it for a moment before pulling it back. And, of course, the much simpler task of sending it from one hand to the other through the frame. She had already tried the walls, the door, and the black glass windows. The only other conductive thing was the door, which seemed to be wood plated with metal.

She was going to have to get out while being walked to a test, probably.

At the end of the day, three more prisoners had been brought in – a Clairvoyant sibling group. Y'Starren had asked them if they were planning to escape, and they paled visibly and stopped chatting altogether. That's why she was silently sitting on her bed practicing while they played chess.

And then there was a sudden bolt sound and the door swung open, revealing several guards, a few technicians, and Yeckswem behind them.

"On the beds!" he ordered.

He didn't have to. The three Clairvoyants had already scurried to them and sat down, eyes closed, hands clenched together on their chests. From their behavior, they were waiting to be hurt. From the taser in Yeckswem's hand, this happened on a regular basis.

"Charger." Yeckswem snapped his fingers.

Y'Starren got up, folding her arms with a small sigh. Her electricity was almost gone, and she was tired.

The technicians were drilling holes in the wall at top speed, guards crowding around the door with batons and tasers ready. Now the technicians yanked her bed over to the wall where they were drilling. Two thin cables of solid metal were now attached to the wall, ending with a pair of cuffs ... her size.

"Sit," Yeckswem ordered.

Y'Starren glanced around once at the other Chazans before deciding to go, promising herself that a better chance would come.

They fastened the cuffs, which were oily inside, to her wrists, and Y'Starren noticed with discomfort that they were not long enough for her to lie down in bed with.

"Wait, you're not going to leave me here all night in these ... "

"All night, every night." Yeckswem smiled slightly at her pleading look.

"Yeckswem, I can't sleep like – "

She was cut off by a roar of the fan from the other side of the room, and suddenly there was a huge draining sensation through the cuffs. She grimaced and slumped over her drawn-up legs, hands dangling on either side. She groaned as her muscles ached, electricity drawn away from her too fast – faster than she could pull it in. Was this what being tased was supposed to feel like?

"It's too much ... I don't have anything left to give," she groaned.

Yeckswem came to her and grabbed her left hand.

"Charge it," he said, adding, "Charge the hand," when she frowned in confusion.

He reached slowly into his pocket with his free hand. She stiffened as he pulled out the line, placing its cold length against the hot blisters down her arm. She heard a shift in the rest of the room as they saw what he'd been making those marks with.

"Do it," he said.

She clenched her jaw and looked away. Permission to hurt him had to be a trap.

Y'Starren felt the electricity run toward him instinctively, only to be cut off mid-flow by the cuff. She closed her eyes to concentrate once more. It didn't work, though she felt a separate flow in her abdomen. That meant that she could definitely separate it in her body, just not that close to the cuff. She needed to practice.

She looked at the line out of the corner of her eye, trembling.

"Well?" he said, lifting it like he was about to hurt her.

"I – I'm sorry – " She felt herself starting to shake. "Please don't hurt me, I'm trying. I'm trying!"

"Try it more."

She did.

Nothing.

She lurched into a sob, pulling at her arm. His grip was so fucking tight around her wrist that it didn't budge an inch. He tapped her burning arm warningly. She shuddered.

"See, I tried, but it's stopping at the cuff. I tried." Tears ran down her cheeks. "I can't – I can't do it."

Slowly he lifted the line. She clenched her jaw and turned her face away, waiting for him to strike her. But he didn't.

He was putting the line back into his pocket, letting go of her hand. He tilted her face up by the chin. She blinked back the crying, gritting her teeth and forcing herself to stop. Her eyes blazed into his defiantly.

"Calm it," he said. "I don't whip you now."

She took a breath for courage, then snapped her teeth at him like a threat to bite. He flinched.

"Fuck off," she said.

His hand turned into a fist, which she expected him to knock into her jaw, but while his eyes flickered with an uncontrolled wrath, he pulled back.

"Will regret it," he said as they left.

Y'Starren closed her eyes and jerked at the very fixed metal cords. She probably would regret it.

***

The next day, Y'Starren was once again strapped to a chair, but this time she was in a place that smelled like a bathroom and had massive windows that looked out into the wild land where the barbarians lived. It was beautiful. For a moment, she let her mind take her away as she waited for whatever horrible treatment was coming.

The forest rose up into the mountains opposite them, with very few treetops reaching above the window. Huge clouds of mist hung over the morning forest, with occasional trails of faraway smoke coming from the mountains.

Out there, some barbarian clan was resting around that fire, stripping fresh meat off a piece of carcass they'd killed recently, or cooking wild potatoes in the coals. Wild potatoes ... you always burn yourself trying to dig the flesh out of the crispy skin, because they take so long to cool, and you are always so hungry. And the way they fill up your stomach is worth the burn.

And then the door opened and she flinched, stomach tensing to the point that her appetite vanished, her mouth dried up in an instant, and she huddled forward, grateful for the curtain of dirty orange braids that hid her flinching face. Her arms were the tensest – scabbed and bruised, she could almost feel the stinging of the line across her skin again.

"Leave us. I don't think she's a threat," the woman said. "I speak a little Bane. How's that?"

She gently touched Y'Starren's shoulder.

Y'Starren flinched hard.

"I'm sorry," she whispered automatically.

The woman's hand retreated quickly.

Y'Starren heard her moving around behind her, dragging a rolling tray closer. She grimaced, keeping her head down under her hair. She looked out from between the braids at the woman. The Chazan had covered her mouth, stepped back a pace, and was looking at Y'Starren's scabbed arm, colored all down the forearm with dull red bruise lines. Her hand shifted on her own mouth as if she wanted to re-cover it and then realized her hand was already there.

"Uh – are you okay?" Y'Starren said.

"Oh. Uh." The woman lowered her hand, looked like she didn't know what to do with it, and then held it out toward Y'Starren, who recoiled slightly. "I'm Yin," she said slowly. "I'm not going to hurt you."

Y'Starren gritted her teeth when she heard that and saw the concerned look the woman was trying to hide. Maybe it was a trick. A test.

"Oh, yeah? Then why am I tied to a chair?" Her voice trembled with fear she couldn't hide. She was glad the woman couldn't see her quivering lips.

The woman reached for something on the tray, and paused when she saw Y'Starren grip the armrests of the chair that her wrists were tied to, knuckles going white.

"I told you I'm not going to hurt you, Charger," the woman said. "Are you going to hurt me?" Y'Starren bit her cheek, trying to calm herself down with a couple breaths.

"Depends on behavior of it," Y'Starren answered like they had answered her, but sarcastically. "Gonna pinch me? Whip me?"

Yin walked around in front of Y'Starren, holding a pair of scissors close to her chest. The gray light from the early morning outdoors wrapped around her body, making her look darker, more ethereal.

Y'Starren wanted to add another sarcastic comment, but when she looked up with hard eyes, she saw a concerned look on Yin. Her lips were slightly parted, and she looked like she was trying to decide what to say.

"Young gifted, I am a barber. I am not going to hurt you," she said slowly. "Do you ... "

"I behend what you're trying to say," Y'Starren rolled her eyes. "But do I believe you?" She shrugged.

Yin sighed and pulled up a chair next to Y'Starren's. As Yin reached for her hair, Y'Starren's arm jerked reflexively at the tie over the chair, but Yin did not hurt her. She wrapped a towel over the girl's shoulders and took a couple of her narrow braids in her hand.

"Don't," Y'Starren whispered, and it came out in a choked sob. "Please, don't cut my hair."

"I'm really sorry," Yin said. "I have to. If I refuse, they'll just find someone else to do it."

Y'Starren moaned, breaking into actual crying.

"Don't cut my hair ... " she cried. "Please, don't cut my hair."

Yin's hands dropped into her lap, and Y'Starren saw a tear drip down the woman's white face. The woman didn't say anything, though she looked like she was trying to and then swallowing instead.

After a minute, Y'Starren managed to stop, blinking tears out of her eyes and sniffling, wiping her face on her shoulders.

" ... It's okay," she said finally. She managed half a shrug. "What do I need my blazing hair for?"

"It's beautiful," Yin said.

Y'Starren laughed, still trying not to cry anymore.

"You think these dirty ropes are beautiful?" She sniffed. "Do you realize how much they itch?" But her eyes teared up again when Yin started cutting them off.

It turned out they did have a machine to make your hair the exact same length all over your head, and it was loud, but it surprisingly didn't hurt at all.

As Yin brushed the extra hair away from Y'Starren's neck, she told her about her boyfriend, who was going to be a guard, so that he could try to work near Yin.

"I will say the haircut took very long, if you want," Yin said, pausing and sitting down. "Less tests."

Y'Starren met her eyes briefly, then tore them away from the painfully kind expression and looked back out the window.

"Less pain," Yin added, more softly, gently touching Y'Starren's hand, which was swollen under the pressure of the wrist restraints. "I'm sorry. I don't think they should treat you this way."

"Yeah?" Y'Starren said.

She was considering asking Yin for help escaping, but her stomach flipped in panic at the very idea. She had to know if she could trust Yin.

"You may be Bane, but you are still human," Yin said. "I think." She frowned.

"You *think*?" Y'Starren repeated.

"It's unethical to ... to whip your subjects," Yin said, biting her lip. "I'm so sorry."

Y'Starren sighed, scraping her nails against the chair arms.

"I've tried reporting them, but ethics don't care as long as results come forth." Yin put the scissors on the tray, and Y'Starren thought about the pliers.

"No qualms about the whole non-consensual part, though?" Y'Starren said.

"Qualms?" Yin asked. "What is it?"

"It's ... you don't think it's unethical to hold Banes here, when we just ... want to fucking go home?"

Yin sighed and got up, pushing her tray away. She came back to Y'Starren and released her ankles, then her wrists. Y'Starren rubbed her wrists and cautiously stood up. Wordlessly she took a broom and swept around the chair where she'd been sitting, collecting orange twists of hair in one pile.

"But ... " Yin stared.

"I just wanted to help," Y'Starren muttered. "Sorry."

Yin picked up a dustpan and took the broom gently from Y'Starren, sweeping the hair up. This stranger, knowing Y'Starren's gift, didn't seem afraid of her at all. It was such a strange, long-hoped-for feeling. Something she'd never thought would happen, and for it to happen here was completely unexpected.

"I thank you," Yin said doubtfully. "Is that how you would say it?"

"Basically." Y'Starren shrugged. She tried to smile, and it came out floppy, so she stopped, wincing instead. "Right. I guess I'll just go back to my torture now?"

Yin cursed under her breath, looked at the clock, and her eyes fell to the ground. The look told Y'Starren that this was probably the longest that Yin would be able to keep Y'Starren away from Yeckswem.

"Just do as they say, and they won't hurt you."

Y'Starren sighed.

"I wish."

***

Week after week, Y'Starren studied every path in the building and every map she could get her hands on. Every door and every lock, and how it was opened.

The nature of the tests and her own obstinance when it came to hiding her secrets resulted in her returning to the prisoners' cell later than everyone else and covered in welts and bruises, some of which would blister only to break the next day when she was whipped across the same spot. The jumpsuit they forced her to wear was cold and didn't protect her at all from the abuse – they had kept it sleeveless and the bottom half didn't even come halfway down her thighs. They'd taken all of her decorative strings and handmade jewelry. And no matter how much she twisted and matted her hair, it wasn't long enough to braid.

It had to be worth it – she had to rescue Wackee, and that would make every extra strike she'd taken to hide her true power worth it. She imagined living with him on the run, somewhere in the wilds. Barely safe, but together. It would be horrible not having their parents there, but there was one last spark of beauty in her life, one last piece of family, and she wasn't going to give up on it. Ever. Not if it got her a hundred lashes. Which it did.

They hooked her up to more and more powerful equipment to see how high her charge could get, then struck her legs till they bled in lines across them and she screamed. They also tried to make her practice taking in and putting out more power, faster, and arcing the electricity further and further from her fingers. Keeping her progress steadily behind where she actually was cost her a lot. The bleeding lines on her legs and the layered bruises could attest to that. Yeckswem probably would've tortured her either way.

But each time, she practiced. She practiced pretending to give them all her magic, while really holding it deep in her abdomen, waiting to strike at the right moment. Waiting to strike when she knew the way out.

She had counted ten weeks since her imprisonment, and she was waking up from nightmares every time she was dragged out of the prisoners' cell. They were nightmares of Wackee being found out, or of Wackee trying to look for her and getting dragged in here, or of her running back for him with a naive smile on her face, only to find him face-down and cold outside the gates of Strangers' College – dead before he even got accepted. That was the most horrible one.

So every time she was released from those painful shackles in the subjects' holding cell, her eyes were already baggy and frightened, strained from unshed tears.

It had been a horrible day, not that that made it special. She had been taken to the chair under the lamps and tested with bigger electrodes, and lashed across her thighs when the output slowed. She'd pushed past the pain and controlled her output anyway, successfully deceiving them about how much she could do. These days, she could gather electricity much faster – she'd been practicing. And she kept that a secret, despite the torture and the tests. They'd left her there in the chair for two hours while they discussed the confusing results, and she had sank into a dreadful, unavoidable sleep while waiting for them to come back and torture her some more. Then they'd come back in, take her somewhere else, and the cycle repeated. Always trying to push her body further, sometimes examining her brain and taking chunks of her flesh to study. They didn't waste anesthetic for that.

She'd spent the first three weeks trying to act compliant – anything to make them whip her a little less. Tired of begging and crying, she found her screams absent of tears these days, ending in silent sobs and shudders.

Every time they took her somewhere else, she kept her eyes down, forcing herself to scan the passageways for the exit. Sometimes she believed it was pointless. She did it anyway. She had to.

Now Y'Starren was being half-dragged along down the hall – she could hardly stand, let alone walk without help – when she caught the golden light of sunset coming in from one of the half-open rooms to the left. She guessed that that was the side of the building that looked out from the face of the cliff. It wasn't much of a clue for how to get out, but it was something. She bit her cheek and tried not to hope too much.

As they walked down the hall, her hands were manacled in corded shackles that attached to a battery that was supposed to "ground" her – draw the charge, for the scientists' safety. Having that much of her charge sucked out weakened her physically. She constantly felt dizzy and sick.

Unknown to them, however, she had been figuring out how to not charge it. After charging this box for a minute, she wouldn't have enough power left to really hurt any of them, though she could still deliver a painful static shock after a minute or two without the manacles. After some private practice on the very conductive bedframe, there was really nothing stopping her from bashing it into someone's head right now and then electrocuting them. Nothing except the strategy she'd chosen.

The fronts of both her legs and arms were covered in welts and dark red lines. Under those were a multitude of darker purple ones. The stab and pinch wounds had healed a long time ago, but a reopened weal on the top of her thigh, one of the worst spots they had targeted that day, was dripping a mixture of blood and some watery substance. It trickled down to her ankle and left tiny spots where her heel touched the floor at each step, and it itched. The scientist that sometimes cleaned up her wounds, Menyth, hadn't seemed to notice this one, and she didn't dare draw attention to them openly. When she did, Yeckswem tended to punish her even more for it. He clearly didn't like the other scientists noticing the marks of his brutality. It was better to ignore it.

As usual, the scientists that passed eyed her openly with a mixture of disgust and concern, though most seemed to be more interested in her charging ability. While Y'Starren had started to see them as sort of ... the same as anybody else, some bad, some good, they clearly saw her as some kind of other-worldly specimen.

As she stepped the last weary step up a flight of stairs, she paused at the top. Suddenly she recognized the hall. Yeckswem was watching her, so she cast her eyes down with her now-typical depressed stare, but stealthily scanned the area through her peripheral vision.

Let this be real ... She cursed under her breath.

"Repeat it." Yeckswem put a hand on her shoulder and tilted her chin up with a jab of his thumb.

She blinked away, refusing to look at him.

"It's nothing," she said, finding her voice hoarse.

He reached for his pocket, where he kept the blazing line.

"I just said 'horizons,'" Y'Starren said in a low voice. "Alright? Gonna whip me for that?"

"Why 'horizons'?" Yeckswem said, pausing with his hand in his pocket.

"It's a Bane ... " She hesitated. He wasn't going to believe her that that was a Bane curse. "It's an idiom for 'I'm tired,'" she said.

He grunted and assented.

There were still too many guards around, and there were two at the door she and Merreth had been let in over two months ago. But the door was there, and she knew where it went. Could she escape this way later? She went over and over in her mind how to get out. Left from the cell, down the hall, take a right, up the stairs, out the door.

Too many variables.

If she was going to escape, she needed to do it now. But she was out of electricity – they'd drained her repeatedly throughout the day. She stared at the door, clenching her fists.

This might be her last chance.

As Y'Starren was trying to strategize, she was unexpectedly shoved sideways into a room and crowded in by an unusually large horde of scientists. And in the room, waiting expectantly by a huge machine and flanked by two guards, was Mainmwim.

There was also a more rudimentary chair, with the ever-present restraints at the armrests and chair legs, and on either side of it was what Y'Starren now recognized as a massive battery with a bunch of cords going out through the wall, and a bunch more going into the computers across the back and middle of the room.

Y'Starren slumped, then fell to her knees on the floor. Her legs ached, her skin stung and burned all down the front of her legs where she'd been struck repeatedly throughout the day, and her hands tingled from how much electricity she'd been forced to push through them. They were blackened on the skin and so tired they were going numb.

She found herself hyperventilating. She couldn't do another test.

"What's wrong?" Mainmwim said.

Y'Starren gritted her teeth and glared at him as he came closer. Someone was about to hurt her and make her get up. But she couldn't get up.

She saw Yeckswem coming from the left and clenched her shoulders as she saw him take the weapon out of his pocket. She gasped as the metal cut across her back. Her cuffed hands shot up to protect her head as she shuddered, waiting for the rest of the whipping.

"Rise, pissant," Yeckswem said.

"But I ... " Y'Starren shuddered, ducking her head again as she said, "I can't stand."

Mainmwim walked closer and reached out a hand in her direction. She stiffened as he put a hand over her forehead, thumb crooking under her eyebrow as he pushed her head back to see her face.

"I asked, what's wrong?" he repeated.

She gritted her teeth, meeting his eyes.

"I can't do any more today," she whispered. "Please. I can't take any more. It won't do any good. I can't do any more."

Her body shook as silent tears ran down her face. When he let her head go, she lifted her manacled hands to cover and wipe her eyes. As she did, the scientists went quiet – usually a clue that they were communicating nonverbally while she was too busy dealing with the effects of whatever they'd last done to her to pay attention.

"Alright." Mainmwim put a hand on her head, which now had the hair cropped short like the other subjects. "You can do it either with or without more pain."

"No." Y'Starren found wrath exploding out of her. "No, I can't! What about 'I can't do it' don't you understand?"

"Give her the line," Mainmwim said.

She choked back a cry as the metal snapped into her bare upper arm, recoiling toward the wall. She shuffled until she was leaning against it, pressing her right arm and temple against it, grimacing. *Snap* – it slit her skin open with a sting that made her scream through her teeth. *Snap. Snap. Snap.* Her screams grated against her throat and rattled the tube-shaped ceiling lights.

"You can either cooperate," Mainmwim was saying. "Or ... " Yeckswem continued to lay into her with the line.

She held her breath. She didn't want to scream. It hurt.

I'm going to kill you, she kept thinking. She used to think about killing them every night, but now she was too tired to feel the old rage. It was just an automatic comfort thought. She'd never be able to kill them.

A harder lash broke her silence, and her scream reached each of the four corners in the ceiling, echoing with each consecutive one.

As he paused, she panic-planned, eyes darting around for resources. And then she saw the test equipment and realized something.

"I'll try!" she screamed. "Fuck you, I never said I wouldn't try!" She sobbed as he hit her again, not stopping.

Her breath sucked in with a choking sound, the tail end of a cry she was trying not to release.

Y'Starren had been practicing, and she knew a few more things about electricity from paying attention to the Chazans, who still assumed that she hadn't picked up on any of the technical jargon they used.

A human could be killed by as little as nine volts as long as there was enough amperage behind those nine. Pulsing the magic could cause some kind of additional danger, though she hadn't figured out exactly what.

And Y'Starren could release magic in a little less than a tenth of a second. As the line cut into her arm again, she focused the magic into it and up into Yeckswem's hand, hitting his thumb and then his upper arm, which jerked back. He let out a cry of pain.

"You dare to – "

Y'Starren struggled to her feet.

"I said I'd try!" she screamed.

Yeckswem gripped the line even tighter now, face looking almost blue with cold rage.

"Penalty of line – " he started, raising it, but Mainmwim cut him off.

"Wrong is you, Yeckswem," he said. "Charges it." He pointed to the chair, addressing Y'Starren now. "Charger, charge it."

Y'Starren knew the drill by now. She groaned and got to her feet painfully, arm throbbing as the movement broke open one of the welts. The scientists closed in around her.

"You don't have to restrain me!" she snapped, grabbing the correct electrodes from each of the batteries, one in each hand. "You want me to charge it? Watch me." *I'll fuckin' charge it alright.*

The battery on the right was full of charge. They were probably going to see how much she could draw from that one, and how quickly. Their experiments had started to revolve around the idea of mimicking her body as a man-made, more controllable biological battery. And they definitely thought she was too stupid to understand that, but she'd picked it up.

And she was going to surprise them.

She took a deep breath, and it shuddered on the way out as she pulsed the tiny bit of electricity left in her body into the empty battery. Scientists were rushing to the panels to watch their little test play out in real time. She found a genuine, though malicious, grin coming naturally to her face for the first time in months.

Then she pulled the charge – every drop of it – into her body in a split second.

Hell yeah.

Back to normal. This was how she'd felt after a week of walking through thunderstorms – though after all this practice, she could probably suck in much more.

She dropped the electrodes and turned around, lifting her hands and spreading her fingers. Electricity jumped over the fingers of each hand.

"No – restrain it!" Mainmwim ordered, backing toward the door. His guards moved toward Y'Starren, and she snapped her fingers at them, glaring into their black eyes with her fiery orange stare.

They hesitated.

"Range of arc is but three inches," Yeckswem said, approaching her with a grim, set look.

As he raised the line to begin whipping her with it, she grabbed his hand and pushed it toward his waist, stepping up to him and looking into his eyes. Then she squeezed and sent the electricity straight through just his thumb. She didn't let go, but sent through three pulses, making him scream.

If a scientist was its own species, its resting state would be one of observation. Y'Starren was counting on this as she watched Yeckswem crumple and the other scientists either pulling out tasers or backing away. Someone was already in the hallway screaming for the guards. Y'Starren strode forward quickly, relying on the intimidation factor.

Two scientists with tasers blocked her way.

"Yeah, go ahead, tase me. I love it," she said.

At their hesitation, she extended both her arms. Looking at each other with disbelief on their faces, they did what she said and the tasers struck into her arms. She sucked the energy in, though it jolted a little harder than Yeckswem's taser. Then she put her hands on both of their shoulders, enjoying their horrified expressions, and shocked them through the necks.

At this point, the other scientists in the room had hastily picked up makeshift weapons.

She pushed the other two out of her way and stumbled right into a rubber-gloved hand on her chest, with several more similarly-clad guards coming up behind them. She'd noticed these suits; they were called hazmat suits and were mostly made out of rubber. She ripped the mask up and plunged her hand into the guard's face, letting out a bolt of electricity so hard that he shot backward with the force, knocking into the other guys and buying her some time to flee.

She absolutely did, running straight for the exit. The guards there actually looked terrified, but they raised what looked like more tasers in her direction.

"Hold! Hold!" Chazans behind her shouted.

That meant to not tase her, which Y'Starren thought was a good idea for them. She ran at them.

"Hurt or pass?" she shouted at them.

"Pass! Pass!" The one on the left scrambled out of the way, but as she took hold of the doorknob, he pushed on the door, beckoning at his companions, who were almost at Y'Starren's heels, squeaking along awkwardly in the hazmat suits. The one she had hit hard was still motionless on the ground.

Don't look back, she told herself. She'd known this would happen. It had to happen.

She hit both guards – slapped them on the hands, sending electricity up hard and fast. And they collapsed. As they fell, she shoved them out of the way, yanking open the door, and when she came outside onto the balcony that she and Merreth had come in by months ago, she jumped over it onto the cement below, and ran into the forest as fast as she fucking could.

***

Y'Starren had been running for only a few minutes before she couldn't anymore. Her lungs burned, and her heart pounded so hard it was the only thing she could feel. And her legs, once welted and bruised, were now also ripped up, practically flayed by the underbrush. She tumbled down and leaned against a tree, legs stinging so bad she almost forgot the pain in her ribs from the stitch in her side.

"You fuckers," she panted through ripped vocal chords. "Fuck you so much."

She lifted a middle finger over her head in their direction, vaguely.

She could still hear them. They had run out after her.

Now, as she sat there panting, she heard this terrible whirring, chopping sound like a hundred knives on cutting boards all at once, and she saw something out of the top of her vision, and looked up. A black thing like a massive bee was up there, flying about a hundred feet overhead.

"Oh, fuck me … " she whispered. "They really can fly."

She was up and running again in a moment, and this time, she lunged down toward the canyons, regardless of what barbarian tribes might be down there using the water.

What started off as a high rocky streamlet, which she tramped alongside as fast as she could go without passing out, got deeper and deeper, till she found herself in a gorge between two cliffs, only going deeper in. She kept going, heart still hammering in her chest.

It was almost more about what she'd left behind than what would happen if she was caught again. Maybe they were still behind her, she thought. She looked back, but there was nothing.

She slowed as she reached a place where the stone above her met. It opened up again a little ahead, so she kept going cautiously. She hated the trapped sensation she was starting to feel. But if they were looking for her from above, maybe this was a good thing.

She finally trudged up to the side of a pool of water that had gathered in a wider place in the canyon, by a tiny drizzling waterfall.

She sat by the fall, dipped her cropped head under it for a moment, and let the cold water run over her face for a wonderful moment. Then she got a headache and had to stop.

Something about cold water always made her feel clearer and happier. It reminded her that there was more to life than whatever funk she was stuck in. Even if they caught her again, even if they dragged her back and used the line on her till she was left with no skin on her at all, she'd still have gotten here. She'd still have gotten to drink waterfall water and sit on the smooth gravel in this tiny oasis of a cave, watching the beautiful ripples and bubbles from the waterfall gushing outward into the pool, which stilled again before it reached her toes. The water was perfectly clear, and the moss that reached out from the wall was soft and cold under her ears. She turned her head and kissed it, then laughed.

She leaned her head against it and closed her eyes, just for a second.

***

When she woke up, she was freezing.

If she didn't get some help, she was going to die of chill and the minor wounds she was covered in. Her legs were like solid rocks that ached like a motherfucker. She wouldn't get very far without food and warmth, but there was no one but barbarians out here.

She tried to get up, and it felt like her skin ripped open all down her legs and arms and she screamed in pain, hitting the rock wall she'd slept against. It burned. Exposing her back to the cold breeze had reminded her of how soaked she was across the back of her scanty jumpsuit. She stared up into the canyon opening at the cold white stars in the black night. It was so cold.

Then she heard voices nearby, and she stiffened. They had that unmistakable throaty accent of the barbarians. She had to get out of here. She tried again to get up, but her weak legs gave out before she got halfway up. She cursed softly, tears springing to her eyes. After all this work, to get bumped off by barbarians … It was just not fair. She dragged herself a little ways away from the waterfall, into the shadows, gritting her teeth and holding her breath every time she moved so she wouldn't cry out in pain.

There were soft splashes as whoever it was waded through the last canyon bottleneck before Y'Starren's hiding place. One of them was holding a torch. She grimaced, leaning her head against the stone.

They spoke softly, moving toward her. They'd obviously heard her and had been close enough to tell that she was nearby. There were two of them, one of them dangling a dead rabbit from his left hand, with knives and arrows stuck into his rope belt. For a moment, she was jealous. They looked so calm, like they really had their lives together. The man to the right with the torch suddenly lowered it and pointed at Y'Starren, who cursed again.

The man raised his eyebrows, lifting a hand toward Y'Starren, then beckoned at her.

"No, thanks, I'm good over here," she said, and her voice betrayed her with a quaver. It was so obvious that she'd cried repeatedly today, and was about to do it again. "Dammit," she squeaked, and her breaths shuddered.

The man handed his torch to his partner. They spoke to each other in soft, guttural tones, slightly different from those of the last Warminds she had come across. Maybe these were a different tribe. She noticed, now that she thought about it, that they had hair. They had chopped it at the sides and then braided all the rest of their hair over the top of their scalp down to the nape.

These must be the Grass People, she thought. She was pretty sure she was in their territory by now, and they certainly weren't Warminds.

The man now showed her his hands, empty, eyes wide as if he was trying to make her understand something. He spoke in a very expressive tone, enunciating clearly, like that was going to help. Unlike the Warmind dialect, not a word of it made a lick of sense to her.

But the man was moving closer, and he reached out and touched her leg gently. She flinched and hissed in pain, and he jerked back, looking at his hand, rubbing his fingers together, then rubbing them on his pants. Looking alarmed, he started speaking more rapidly both to his friend and to her, then stood up, reaching out a hand to her insistently, shaking it and beckoning with his fingers when she hesitated. His tone wasn't threatening, but neither was Yeckswem's half the time.

She didn't want to go, but it was better than dying here, which she knew she would do if she didn't get some help.

She took the hand, and nearly collapsed after she was on her feet. He looped an arm around her back and pulled her toward the light, supporting her every time she stumbled.

Bare feet slipping on the rocks, they guided her out of the canyon.

As she walked, the stone evened out under her. In some places, the stone felt like it had been chipped into the shape of stairs here and there, and gravel and moss had been scuffed away to create an easy way to walk up and out of the canyon.

As they did, she heard a pleasant sound – the sound of laughing, and an old man humming. Then the man would snort with laughter, pause, and begin singing again. People were talking softly at the top of the canyon.

On top of the bluff over the river, barbarians sprawled around a fire, many on bedrolls made of skins and woolen blankets. There was a small cabin off a ways into the forest, embraced by a rocky outcropping above it.

Grass surrounded the worn places near the fire, and a couple children that looked to be about eight and ten were playing there by the bluff.

Y'Starren slipped and nearly fell to her knees on the way there, but the barbarian caught her, making a comment to his partner, who just grunted a single-syllable response.

In the light of the fire, her bright orange hair and eyes would be much more visible. She waited for someone to point at it, call her a witchling, and get ready to sacrifice her, but none did.

As her features were illuminated, their eyes grew round and excited, and they pointed to her. Even the man carrying her squinted at her, touched her hair, and looked down into her eyes, but then she staggered and nearly fell. He barely caught her, saying the same word – "Duilagh-duilagh" – several times like an apology.

Somehow she expected to hear someone cursing at her for falling and feel the line cutting into her skin. She jerked around, thinking she heard it hiss behind her. A moment later, she realized she was hyperventilating, staring into the barbarian's eyes as he stroked her cheek, saying something gently.

He lowered her onto a pile of blankets close to the fire, which someone that looked very much like him, probably his little brother, rolled off of for him.

Her eyes widened, but she was getting dizzy and her hands were clammy and cold. The cuts all over her body had given her a fever again. This wasn't the first time her injuries had led to a fever, but this was the first time someone had looked startled and concerned instead of pissed at her for it.

"Look, I didn't mean to," she said, trying to get up, but the barbarian pushed her back onto the blankets, saying something else. "I'll get out of your hair. I know barbarians don't like weaklings."

The barbarians responded in their foreign dialect as if they were having a normal conversation.

She turned her face away, mind a whirling mixture of relief and terror, curling in on the less cut-up side of her body. She felt slightly less vulnerable when she looked into the fire.

The barbarians let out a laugh, with an "Ah!" The way people sound when they say "Called it!"

The man who had helped carry her back sat down near her with his little brother, while his friend with the meat took it away somewhere. The man touched her hair, and she flinched, hands close together like they had been in the manacles so that they didn't yank and bruise the wrists. That was going to be embarrassing till she could break that habit.

"Sh-sh-sh ... " He stroked her hair comfortingly.

"Don't touch the hair." She shivered.

She realized she was trembling like a leaf. Probably the chill.

He spoke to her while some of the others gathered around, and the others went back to their conversations, though their eyes drifted to her with a great amount of curiosity. These people were blazing tall, she noticed, with powerful-looking legs and chests. The young man who had carried her up had a wispy, cropped beard and a quick smile that vanished the moment he focused back on Y'Starren.

He showed her a piece of cotton cloth – clearly a rarity here, since everyone except her was dressed in either wool or skins – and a small kettle of steaming water, and told her something about all that, then asked, "Gu leor?"

"Look, man, I speak Bane," she said.

He said more words, then asked again – "Gu leor?"

Biting her cheek, she shrugged doubtfully in response. Then he put the cloth on her leg and she flinched and grabbed his hand.

"Like I can't clean my own wound," she said.

He started pointing and talking about the different cuts on her body, asking his tribe members about it, and they came closer, eyes widening as more wounds were revealed.

Y'Starren only realized she was slipping into some kind of dazed sleep when she felt the touch of the cloth on her leg and she flinched.

"Blazes," she whispered.

"Duilagh," he said.

He wasn't rough – in fact, he was gentler than her own mother would've been, and spoke softly as he cleaned her wounds with his brother's help. Occasionally he chuckled and bantered with his brother. As he wiped dirt that was stuck to the wounds on the tops of her legs, he asked her questions. She gathered he was asking why she was so injured.

"Because some people don't have a conscience," she said.

He replied with a few bemused words.

"I don't know, do you?"

He looked at her with an odd smile, then shook his head and chuckled. She smiled. Neither of them understood each other.

Finally, he sighed and tossed the cloth onto the grass, pouring some of the warm water from the kettle on his hands to rinse them. He smiled at her, then looked up at the sky, leaning back onto his elbows. He made a comment that sent his brother into a fit of giggles.

Y'Starren's shudders of pain and terror had decreased to slower breaths now, and her tired heart beat slower and slower as she leaned back, wrapping the wool blankets around herself. She fell asleep to the sound of the tribe members talking around her.

***

Y'Starren spent another week there with the tribe. They didn't seem to mind that she was a Bane or a witchling. They didn't seem to care what she did, but simply shared their food when they ate, offered her water, and let her sleep in the extra blankets by the fire until her wounds were so healed that they were down to lines of scabs and green and purple bruises. Her skin didn't burn and sting anymore, though now that she wasn't being beaten across the healing skin, she could see a pattern of slanting red scars down her arms and legs.

She fended off those thoughts as she walked away, wearing the new wool tunic they'd insisted on giving her before she left. She didn't understand, but she bowed many times to them and swore to them in her own language that if she could ever help them in return, she would.

Now if she wanted to make it back to Baneon before Wackee was expelled and forced to go to Wenterglen, she had to walk all night and all day without stopping. She would get to Seechatee in the late night tomorrow, and take a night's rest and beg some food off them. They'd probably remember her and give her something.

The entire night, as she walked above the river on the same path Merreth had taken her by before, she imagined what would happen if everything went wrong. She kept trying to tell herself to focus, but all she could think was what could happen.

She took a massive detour around the Warmind territory and left the riverbank, having no flask and no food, hoping to still reach Seechatee that night.

By dusk, her legs were giving out every few minutes, and she had to stop.

***

Woken up by raindrops falling on her bare legs, Y'Starren got up as the grayest blues of morning were peeking up in the east. It rained all through the early hours, hard. She was soaked through the dirty outfit they'd made her wear at the facility, not to mention the thick woolen tunic laying over that. She forced herself to walk quickly to stay warm.

As she strode into Seechatee, she recognized a couple of kids that noticed her, pointed, and then ran. Her family had been at Seechatee last, and she couldn't help passing through the town on her way – she needed some food and water, at least. And a cloak would go a long way, if anyone was that kind.

The ten or so cottages in Seechatee crushed upward into the mountainside like they were trying to get away from the road, which doubled as a flash flood zone right now. Bare feet slipping through the rocky mud, she sighed as she plodded up the hill toward the homes that doubled as tiny shops. She was standing in what was essentially a river as the townspeople all kind of gathered around her, frowning and muttering amongst themselves.

"Alright, I know it wasn't all melons and roses when we left, but let's not start off angry," she said.

A man pointed at her and she flinched, then clenched her fist. She wasn't going to let people hurt her anymore.

"You're supposed to be dead," he said.

" ... Excuse me?" Y'Starren said. "Are you the one that blazing reported us?"

"Looks dead enough," another villager said. She was the baker.

"I am not dead!" Y'Starren protested.

"What are you doing, walking in here bald, half-naked – " The baker's eyes wandered to her legs momentarily, disgusted. "And blazing ... not dead?"

"Horizons ... " Y'Starren glared. "All I wanted was a little bit of water. Is that too much to ask?" Apparently it was. They were balling up fists, grabbing weapons, and moving toward her.

"Still a reward out," someone called. "Do this village a favor and get rid of the Kill Touch before she gets strong enough to kill us too."

Y'Starren's heart pounded hard, but she raised her hand over her head. She was terrified. She snapped her fingers, electricity cracking against her hand like the tail of a whip. It didn't hurt her, but it sure would hurt them.

"I am strong enough to kill you," Y'Starren shouted. "Now back off. I don't want to hurt you."

She really didn't. There were a few teenagers in the crowd, and one kid that couldn't have been more than ten years old. She didn't want to have to choose between her life or theirs.

But instead of backing off, the baker ran at her with a pitch-fork and the tip slammed into her gut, knocking her onto her knees. It was dull, so it probably only made a harsh bruise, but it still hurt like fuck. She gasped for breath, struggling as she was lifted from her hands and knees in the mud by the arms.

"We need that reward money," someone sighed resignedly.

"I don't understand!" Y'Starren shouted. "Why would there be a reward out? I'm an investigator!"

"It's the investigators is lookin' for you," the man on her right said.

The muddy incline was now absolutely full of people, and the rain was pelting down harder and harder again as she was dragged in front of the village elder.

Y'Starren had a lightning ball in her stomach that she was gripping onto with all her might.

The village elder was only about forty, a perfectly bald man with a long beard and a massive build. He squinted down at Y'Starren.

"Elder?" Y'Starren scoffed. "More like younger."

He punched her in the stomach, and she would've fallen if the guys on either side of her hadn't held her up by the arms. She choked in a breath and struggled to stay on her feet. Apparently banter didn't work with these people either. She missed people that appreciated her jokes.

"Keep that tongue in check," the elder said. "Or you'll get a beating."

"Or you could just control yourself."

"That's it." He straightened up. "We're delivering you dead. Martha, get me my spear!"

Y'Starren ground her teeth, taking one last look around at the villagers. There were about twenty-five of them, most older than ten, but there was a kid that looked like he was about eight. If it wasn't for the hope of saving Wackee, she'd have let them kill her. But ...

"Fine," she whispered. "You asked for it."

She ground her feet into the rivulet of a road and channeled her magic down. "I'll try not to kill you."

The electricity from the battery plus nine days of collecting magic eased out from her feet and into everyone standing in the middle of the rain-soaked village.

They screamed and some fell to their knees. Nobody was touching her now.

"She's trying to kill us!" someone screamed.

"If I was trying to kill you, you'd be dead," she growled. This time, she wasn't bluffing.

They staggered toward her.

Suddenly she felt an unusual amount of clarity and calm. She felt like she was surrounded by a bunch of children. And then she was punched in the gut. Hard.

Power exploded out of every part of her body as the pain hit, then the panic and nausea took her to her hands and knees. It was all too much to focus past. She couldn't pull the magic back – she was too disoriented to make it obey her.

When she finally managed to stop it, she looked up from her position on all fours, choking in painful, tiny breaths. They were all on the ground – all over the road in the mud and rivulets. The baker. The young man she now recognized as the barber. She ran a hand through her short, damp hair, remembering the Chazan barber for a moment.

Up and down the road from her, the citizens of Seechatee lay either seizing and going blue, or just completely still. She clutched at her throat, trying not to puke.

What have I done? she thought.

She stood up slowly, rubbing the mud off her hands and onto her bare thighs.

"Anybody else?" she shouted.

Her voice echoed off the mountains behind her. She stepped forward toward the elder's house.

Might as well loot.

***

Y'Starren pulled her cloak further over her face as she waited at the gate of Strangers' College. It was a massive castle, with brilliant lights in a huge plaza down the road, and the walls were black and sharp against the sky.

"Oh, good, she's still here," she heard the guard mutter nervously. "Yeah, she's right over there – " he started to call to someone else, when a boy with spiky orange hair rushed past him with an excited whoop, and dashed out the barred side door, and embraced Y'Starren so hard it took her breath away and pressed in on old bruises.

She'd told them she was looking for Wackee, and that's all she'd told them. Somehow, without seeing her face, he'd known who she was.

She wrapped her arms around him.

Months of hoping for this moment had made it seem unreal. Impossible, even.

The sensation of his smaller body wrapped around hers was completely different.

But he still smelled like rain and dog, as always.

"You're alive." He let go just as suddenly, eyes shiny with a frank smile on his face. "I thought ... "

He was supposed to be angry – she'd told him she was just going to get a job in Wenterglen, and then had disappeared for almost three months.

"You're not mad at me?" she said.

"Why would I be mad?" He frowned, putting his hands on his hips.

Y'Starren narrowed her eyes at him, knowing he tended to say much less than he was thinking. He should definitely be mad at her. Their parents had died, and then she had immediately abandoned him. His face showed no resentment, and no grief either. He appeared as clear and cheery as he always had been.

"Might as well not give you a reason," she said. "Wanna walk?" He shrugged and followed her.

"Wait – you can't just – it's past closing," the guard stammered.

"Come on, Lackee, you know you love me." Wackee winked at him.

Her brother was charming as hell. He knew it, and he used it. The guard grumbled and sat down to wait till they got back.

"So, I heard you were wanted ... " Wackee said.

Y'Starren shook her head and smiled.

"You always hear things you have no right to know about."

The path pushed them closer together as they walked through a damp-smelling cleft in the mossy rock. Sunlight caught them full in the face on the other side. Wackee still hadn't spoken after several minutes, so Y'Starren finally broke the silence.

"It's okay, you know," she said.

He didn't respond.

" ... If you're mad," she added.

He sent her a small smile and stepped forward down onto the rocky trail.

"I told you, I'm not mad."

"Yeah, but I ... "

"Let's go this way." He turned off the road and led her up a leaf-covered, rocky hill that was difficult for her travel-worn feet to grip. Hearing her panting, he reached back a hand to help her. His hands had gotten bigger – he'd bulked up a bit, actually. "Look. I want to show you."

Climbing up onto the rocks at the top of the hill, she was able to look down into the ravine they'd just climbed out of. It was getting a little dark, so the area below looked creepy and magical – the bases of the trees were black, the mist blue, and the bits of sunlight left over as it set graced the branches, turning them all gold.

"No matter how long I stay here, the glamor of the forest is gone," he said, sitting down on the stone and dangling his feet off, kicking them a little. "And I don't know how to find it again."

Y'Starren sat down next to him, looking at him out of the corner of her eye. She could see him, staring into the darkness and looking anxious. Sad. Then he looked up at her with that half-forced smile.

"I'm sorry for not coming back," she said softly. "I tried. I was afraid of bringing assassins down on you."

"I figured." He shrugged. "Let me guess. You were trying to protect me." He glanced at her bare arms and winced. Y'Starren knew they were visibly scarred and still bruised. "That looks like somebody hurt you pretty bad. Tell me you killed 'em."

"I ... I'm not sure," she said. "It really doesn't matter. I got away."

He pursed his lips and scowled into the darkness.

"Fine. I'll kill 'em for you."

Y'Starren huffed. She hoped he wouldn't try something like that, and she certainly wasn't going to enable it.

"Here," she said. She reached into a stolen purse and pulled out a stolen coin pouch. She opened it, gold coins spilling out into her palm. "Use this to pay your tuition."

He frowned. " ... Are you coming to school too, then?"

She shook her head, standing up and dusting her hands off.

"No," she said. "People know I exist. If it gets out to the guild in Wenterglen, I'm toast. I have to wait for all this to blow over."

"All this, meaning?"

Y'Starren really didn't want to tell him that she'd accidentally massacred an entire village. She looked down at her toes, scraping lichen off the rock with her feet.

"I guess you'll hear about it eventually," she said.

Wackee stood up with a very sober expression, looking like he was trying to read her face.

"So, you're going to leave me again?" he said.

She clenched her teeth.

"I'm sorry," she said. "I don't want you to be lonely ... like me."

He wrapped her tightly in his arms. She didn't want him to let go, squeezing him back.

"Come back to me, okay?" he said, voice breaking.

"Fuck, I ... " She felt a tear fall down her cheek. "I will."

ABOUT THE AUTHOR

Havilah has been writing whump since she was a child, to cope with abuse, trauma, and her autism. She writes to shed light on patterns of abuse and underlines the courage of those who endure through suffering and recovery. She portrays heroic survivors to send a powerful message: You are beautiful.

— • —

BEFORE YOU GO

This is the eighth book in 12 Months of Whump, a series of whumpy novellas published by WPP throughout 2025. Each novella can be read as a standalone.

To stay up to date with the 12 Months of Whump series and other whumperfly-inducing projects, visit us at https://thewhumpyprintingpress.tumblr.com/